Christina Maria Schweiger

THE SWAPPED MAN

(Aiden McGilles)

The book

World War 1 Ireland 1916
Young Aiden McGilles falls into the clutches of British soldiers roaming Ireland to recruit young men to fight on the Western Front in Flanders, France.

It is not until he is exposed to the incredible horror of war on the front lines that he realizes he will never return to his family in Ireland.

When he falls injured into a bomb crater under the great Battle of the Sommé, he encounters the German soldier Franz v. Letten, who is lying badly injured in the bomb crater and struggling to die.

Aiden quickly realizes that Franz is not an enemy, but a friend who, in the last hours of his life, makes him an incredible proposal to give him, Aiden, a chance to escape the cruelty of war.

Aiden sees no other way out and agrees. Thus begins for him an adventurous and dangerous journey.

Author

Christina Maria Schweiger was born in 1965 and works as a secretary at the office of a hotel. Her passions are social projects such as hospice and grief worker and writing. Since 2007 she has been working as an author. She has already published a trilogy of novels as well as a village chronicle of her hometown.

Christina Maria Schweiger

THE
SWAPPED
MAN

Novel

Bibliographic Information of the German National Library

The German National Library lists this publication in the Deutschen Nationalbibliothek; detailed bibliographic information is available on the Internet at

http://dnb.d-nb.de.

©December 2020 Christina Maria Schweiger, 1st ed.
©November 2021 English version 1. 1st ed.
Production and publishing house: BoD - Books on Demand, Norderstedt
Research: Michael Whelan
Editing: Stefan Schweiger, Lena O´Neill,
Christina Schweiger
Cover design: Stefan Lindner, Christina Schweiger
ISBN: 9783753498638

ON HURTING GROUND

Poetic Silhouettes

On soldiers, history, love and tragedy

By

Michael J. Whelan

On Hurting Ground
That membrane
The dusty soil
Keeps departed souls
Loved ones
Disconnected
An echoing earth
Repository of broken bones
Separated
We long for them
Those gone before
To reconnect
Like those who live
Once more to walk
On hurting ground

In memory of all fallen soldiers and those who survived the cruelty of war.

The poppy is a reminder of the fields of Flanders, reddened by the blood of the soldiers of the First World War, in reference to the poem "In Flanders Fields" by the Canadian John McCrae. In addition, at that time on the freshly raised hills of the soldiers' graves, the first thing to begin to bloom was the corn poppy.

(source: wikipedia: remembrance poppy)

The Leprechaun

In a shady nook one moonlit night,
A leprechaun I spied
In scarlet coat and cap of green,
A cruiskeen by his side.
Twas tick, tack, tick, his hammer went,
Upon a weeny shoe,
And I laughed to think of a purse of gold,
But the fairy was laughing too.
With tiptoe step and beating heart,
Quite softly I drew nigh.
There was mischief in his merry face,
A twinkle in his eye;
He hammered and sang with tiny voice,
And sipped the mountian dew;
Oh! I laughed to think he was caught at last,
But the fairy was laughing too.

As quick as thought I grasped the elf,
"You're fairy purse," I cried,
"My purse?" he said, "tis in her hand,
That lady by your side."
I turned to look, the elf was off,
And what was I to do?
Oh! I laughed to think what a fool I'd been,
And, the fairy was laughing too.

Robert Dwyer Joyce 1830-1883

Prologue

Ireland 1905

Calbhach and the golden coin

It happened many, many years ago.

The year was 1905 and was slowly drawing to a close. The day began gloomy and grey. Hardly any light penetrated the thick clouds of mist that had been drifting over the green, hilly area of the Hills of Tara since early morning.

In the midst of this lush, green hilly landscape of today's province of Leinster, County Meath in Ireland, at the top of the Hill of Tara, on the hill, a so-called fairy hill, stood an old wooden bench, weathered by much rain, well hidden under a low-growing tree.

A little man was sitting on this bench. He didn't seem to be affected by the rain and the cold and wet weather. No, on the contrary. He lolls on the bench with a satisfied expression on his face. He had just woken up from a short nap.

The male was very elegantly dressed in a green doublet over which he wore a brown waistcoat. On his head was a huge green hat, which he pulled deep into his wrinkled forehead. A bulbous nose stood out, as did the reddish-brown beard that framed the lower part of his face. A long grey pipe protruded from his thick-lipped mouth, from which thick smoke poured out as soon as he pulled on it.

He just stretched his stocky short legs and examined his elegant shoes, which were made of fine brown leather and emblazoned with a brightly polished golden clasp on the top.

He looked proudly at his new shoes. He had only finished them yesterday. Like many other Leprechauns, Calbhach was a shoemaker.

With a contented sigh, he picked up the bottle of whiskey that stood on the bench next to him, took a big swig, and belched contentedly after the whiskey had coagulated warm and burning through his throat towards his stomach.

Yes, that's the way to live,' thought Calbhach and let his arms sink down on the bench beside him, lazily and contentedly. But he had not remembered that just before he had fallen asleep, he had placed his two precious coins next to him on the bench. Before that, he had polished them, as he often did, and looked at them proudly, which he loved to do.

Now, in his carelessness, he had nudged the coins off the bench with his hand and before he could react and reach for them, they were already rolling down the hill. The big silver coin in front and the golden one followed at a short distance. Calbhach jumped up from the bench and rushed excitedly down the hill after his coins. But as the leather of his new shoes was still very stiff and the sole very slippery, it was not at all easy for Calbhach to find a secure grip with his shoes in the wet grass. He slipped again and again, throwing his short, stocky arms up in the air to keep his balance and avoid falling.

Cursing and swearing, he ran stumbling and sliding down the hill, not taking his eyes off his two coins despite the effort. They did not let themselves be slowed down or stopped by the long grass, but rolled down the hill faster and faster in an upright posture. Even when it became flatter and the hill turned into a green, flat meadow, they kept on rolling.

Calbhach just reached the bottom of the hill and tripped so badly over a stone that he did two somersaults head first before he could lie on his side and thus stop his rapid fall.

For a short moment he lay there completely dazed. But after a few seconds he thought of his coins and he quickly jumped up and ran on.

'*Damn* é arís!' he kept shouting angrily in Gaelic, which meant '*Damn it*', waving his short arms wildly in the air as if he could use them to make the coins stop.

Again and again he stumbled with his new, not yet broken-in shoes. As beautiful as he found them, he just regretted not wearing his old, well-worn shoes, with which he would certainly have been much faster.

But he had no choice and didn't care how many times he fell. Again and again he jumped on his short, stocky legs and kept running after his coins. They were very valuable to him, as they were to every other leprechaun. Each of the coins had a special, special gift.

The silver one, for example, could be spent by its owner as often as he wanted, it would always return to his hands and thus grant him eternal wealth.

The golden coin had the special gift of freeing its owner from difficult situations. With this coin you always find a way to follow the right intuition so that true miracles could happen.

Calbhach felt panic rising in him at the thought that he would not find his coins again, or that someone else would find them and take them. He, Calbhach, would be lost. How could he survive in this harsh, hard world without his treasure, without the protection of the coins?

All this flashed through his mind while he was still running. He had long since lost sight of his coins, having fallen too many times. He followed the slight indentation in the damp grass left by the coins as they rolled on tirelessly.

A little way down the slope, Calbhach suddenly saw a small, old, very dilapidated cottage standing directly in the alignment of the coins' path. Calbhach hoped so much that would the coins finally stop there.

When he arrived at the cottage, breathing heavily, he saw that a small, blond boy was sitting on the floor in front of the door, playing with a small piece of wood in the damp, brown mud. This piece of wood functioned for him as a kind of hammer, because with it he kept hitting something of a shiny nature that flashed out of the brown mud.

Calbhach stopped abruptly and was about to shout out loud when he thought better of it. He did not want to frighten the boy.

If the boy lured his parents out of the house by shouting and they discovered the two coins on the boy, his chances of ever getting them back would be even slimmer.

The families here were very poor, they would stop at nothing to get their hands on some money or gold. And everyone in Ireland knew that if they came across a leprechaun, gold and silver would not be far away, just like whiskey and tobacco.

It wasn't often that you got to see a leprechaun, and if you ever did encounter one, you wouldn't let it out of your sight, let alone escape. Because only then, only then will you become it manage to elicit from the leprechaun the secret of the place where the treasure of gold lay hidden. As the legend says, this mysterious place was at the end of a rainbow.

That is why the goblins are reluctant to stay near inhabited houses or places.

But Calbhach had no other chance now. He had to approach the boy diplomatically and calmly coax the two coins from him.

His plan turned out to be very difficult. The boy only noticed Calbhach when he was already standing right in front of him. Curious, but not afraid, he looked at the little male.

"Who are you?" the boy asked curiously, continuing to pound the two coins in the mud, causing them to sink further and further into the soft earth.

"My name is Calbhach," the male replied outwardly friendly, but inwardly trembling with excitement.

 "And who are you? And how old are you?" the male asked hypocritically.

"My name is Aiden and I am six years old. But tomorrow is my birthday and I'll be seven. " he says excitedly.

"Aha... aha... aha! Nice little fellow you are. "

Calbhach thought feverishly about how best to talk about the two coins.

It was a quirk of Calbhach to comment on everything with his 'aha..aha..aha'.

"Aiden, aha. aha. aha. so, you're not cold out here?" he began his conversation cautiously.

The boy was only wearing a half-tattered grey jacket that had more holes than there was fabric to be seen.

Aiden looked up at him briefly and shook his head.

"Are your parents not at home?", Calbhach continued to question him.

"No, they've gone into town, but they should be home soon," little Aiden told him candidly.

"And you're home all alone?"

"No, my sister is still here, she's making dinner."

"Aha aha aha...Shit...So, so!" he fretted, still frantically thinking of how he could take the coins from the boy without him making a fuss.

"Are you a goblin?" the boy asked, looking curiously at Calbhach, then dug the two coins out of the mud, took each in one hand and stood up.

When Calbhach saw the boy holding the two coins in his hands, he was startled and wanted to grab them quickly, but the boy was quicker and put the two coins in his pocket without cleaning them.

"What have you got there?" asked Calbhach hypocritically, as if he did not know that these were his coins.

Aiden looked at him suspiciously. There was no way he was going to give up his treasure, which had rolled into his life so easily. And as he had guessed from his parents' stories, there was a goblin, a leprechaun, standing in front of him.

Aiden was not afraid of the little male. He actually looked quite friendly, he thought to himself.

Calbhach decided to talk to the boy quite honestly and tell him that what he had found there belonged to him. And would then insist that he had to give him back the two coins.

"Little boy. Those things you found there, those are my coins. They rolled off that hill up there and I couldn't catch them until they ended up with you. But now I've found them and you'll give them back to me, won't you?" and he made a droll face.

Aiden looked at Calbhach irresolutely. He sank his dirty hand into his trouser pocket and slowly took out the two coins.

Again and again he looked from the coins to Calbhach and back again. He did not know what to do and tears came to his eyes.

Calbhach saw his sad and disappointed look and pity spread through his otherwise very selfish heart.

He would simply get a new golden coin from his treasure chest.

"You know what, my boy? You give me back the silver coin and you can keep the gold coin.

What do you think, is that a deal?" he suggested to little Aiden, visibly touched.

The latter pondered with childlike seriousness and kept looking wistfully at the two coins. Finally he raised his eyes to Calbhach.

"All right, then I'll give you back the silver coin," Aiden replied hesitantly, and he handed Calbhach the silver coin, but he immediately put the gold one back in his trouser pocket.

"Thank you little boy. Always keep this coin safe and always carry it with you. And if one day you should be in need or find yourself in a difficult situation, take this coin in your hand and it will help you, whatever may happen."

"Thank you dear Leprechaun!" he called out joyfully to Calbhach in response.

At that moment, the red-painted front door of the small cottage opened and his sister called loudly for Aiden.

He turned to her.

"Look, Eimear!", excitedly he pointed with his hand in the direction of Calbhach. But he had disappeared. Aiden looked around irritated.

"What do you want me to see?" his sister asked impatiently.
"Come on in and wash your hands. Mummy and Daddy will
be right back."
Aiden's gaze was still searching in vain for Calbhach, while
he held his gold coin, his treasure, in his left hand, which he
had buried in his pocket.
"Oh nothing. I'm coming," he called out to his sister, with
a mysterious smile on his face and the knowledge,
that he had just met a goblin who had given him a gold coin.
And he would always remember Calbhach's words and
cherish the coin and always carry it with him.

Ireland, Hill of Tara March 1916

Aiden Mc Gilles

Aiden quickly slipped on his brown woollen waistcoat. He wanted to help his parents in the field to round up the sheep. It was an unusually mild March and the animals were already spending a lot of time in the pastures around the cottage.

He quickly finished his cup, even though the tea had already gone cold, when there was a wild knock on the door of the cottage.

Aiden ran to the door in surprise at the energetic and impatient knocking. Who could that be? They very rarely got visitors out here.

Eimear was in Dublin for a few days to sell sheepskins. She was able to stay with an aunt and enjoyed these days very much and the freedom to spend time alone in the city and hoped to meet a man there soon.

When Aiden opened the door, there were several soldiers from the British army, as he recognised from their uniforms. Among them was a neighbour's boy named John.

Proud and excited, he explained that he had decided to follow the British soldiers and the British army into the war. And if he came along, he could also fight in the Irish 16th Division formed under Major General W.B. Hickie.

The 16th Division of Irish Volunteer Recruits marched into France in December 1915 to support the British there.

But they needed a constant supply of 'human weapons', as they called it.

And so they were again on their way across the country to mobilise new soldiers and take them with them to France to join the large-scale British-French offensive against the German positions planned for 1 July 1916, which would eventually also contest the planned, large-scale battle at the Sommé, one of the soldiers explained to him.

Aiden had already heard that British soldiers were on their way to Irish shores. As many Irish as possible should join the British to go into battle together.

The independence movement 'Irish Volunteers', founded in 1913, was now divided into two camps. While the founders of the movement had fundamentally rejected recruitment to Ireland to replenish the British army, the majority, almost 70% of the Irish Volunteers now supported the war against Germany and allowed themselves to be commanded by the British.

So the British haggled for every Irish volunteer they could recruit.

It did not matter whether these young men were inexperienced in combat. From the age of 17 they were considered fit for military service and were sent to the front completely unaware and not sufficiently trained in weapons.

Aiden listened attentively and with interest as the British soldiers spoke to him in glowing terms of the service and honour he would be contributing to his country and also to Britain by going to war with them.

The soldiers explained to him that he would first be trained in arms and only then fight at the front.

Aiden let himself be drawn more and more into this spell of the soldiers' dazzling words.

His parents were in the field at the time and he told the soldiers that he would like to discuss this with his parents first.

One of the soldiers then grabbed him roughly by the arm.
"If you want to be there, then you have to come right away.
We don't have time to wait for you until tomorrow," he
shouted urgently to Aiden, putting him under pressure.
"Pack up a few things. You won't need much. You'll get your
uniform and equipment from the British Army. We'll let
your parents know on the field and you can say goodbye
there."
Aiden felt a little queasy in his stomach. What should he do?
On the one hand, he would be very happy to join and he
would be able to prove himself in the fight of war for his
country. In his youthful inexperience of all things violent and
warlike, he never grasped the magnitude of this decision. He
only saw the glory and honour he could win and then
proudly return to his homeland, Ireland, as a hero.
But on the other hand, he remembered that he could not
leave his parents alone with all the work in the fields.
His father had been very sickly for a long time and often
could not get up from bed all day.
Then Aiden had to be here and take over his father's work.
And besides, what would his mother say?
While he was still struggling with himself to make a decision,
the soldiers pushed him more and more until he finally gave
in and had allowed himself to be so blinded that he went into
his chamber and hastily stuffed some clothes into his old
canvas bag.
He looked down at himself. He was wearing old, patched
trousers and a grey-striped shirt, which was also torn at the
sleeves.
But apart from his Sunday suit, he had nothing to wear that
was presentable.

He reached for his sturdy shoes and his woollen jacket. When he was already at the door, he suddenly stopped, turned around again and looked at his bed.

He walked up to it, knelt down and pulled out an old tin from under the bed. Aiden opened the tin and took out the golden coin that was inside. He looked at it for a moment and remembered again when it had rolled at his feet many years ago, while playing outside the cottage.

He still remembered the little man with the green duster who stood in front of him and wanted the coins back.

Aiden knew he hadn't been dreaming, although when he went to introduce him to his sister Eimear, the goblin was no longer in sight.

But the goblin even told him his name and had given him this golden coin and told him that he should always carry this coin with him, as it will bring him luck and would always free him from any situation, no matter how hopeless.

Aiden thought of that now at this moment and smiling, he put it in his pocket. He would always carry the coin with him and he trusted that it would bring him luck and protect him. Then he went back to the soldiers who were already waiting for him outside the door and they set off for the fields.

*

His mother cried out in despair when Aiden came towards her in the field with the soldiers. He didn't have to say anything, she knew what had happened. Tearful, she fell around his neck and begged him not to follow the soldiers voluntarily. His father just stood there silently, looking into his son's eyes.

"You have to do what you have to do, son. Don't disgrace your country," was all he said. He knew he could not stop him, as hard as it was for him.

Aiden looked over his mother's shoulder, still hanging on his neck, at his father. He could not assess what he was really thinking. His face looked expressionless.

Aiden would have wished in that brief moment, soaked in emotion, that his father had stopped him. But the moment passed and not another word was spoken. Apart from his mother's desperate crying, the field was dead silent.

The soldiers now impatiently called for haste and roughly pulled the mother away from her son.

Tears came to Aiden's eyes, but he didn't want to show his face to the soldiers and bravely swallowed the sudden panic, straightened up and ran after the soldiers who were already hurrying away. He did not turn around. He heard his mother crying and wailing loudly and his heart threatened to burst.

*

West Front/ France 1916

The Irish recruits were first brought from Ireland to England on a large cargo ship, where they remained in a camp for a fortnight and were taught how to shoot and handle the various weapons in a makeshift manner.

At the end of April, Aiden was sent to the Western Front in France with many thousands of soldiers to support the French against the German Army by helping to build front line trenches and ammunition dumps.

Before the trip to France, they were all shaved bald and Aiden's reddish-blond mop of hair fell to the muddy ground below. When he looked in the mirror, he hardly recognised himself.

His big blue eyes looked much bigger than usual and his fair skin, with the pale pink freckles spreading down his nose to his cheeks, stood out much more without hair. His whole face seemed sunken, as he had already lost quite a bit of weight.

The hard work and meagre food rations played their part.

More and more, during those weeks when he worked near the front line in the newly dug trenches and saw many wounded and cruelly mutilated soldiers, he became aware of what he had gotten himself into.

Most of the soldiers around him were also rookies and not much older than him.

But he could not share this eagerness to fight, which many underlined with motivated battle cries. Some days he no longer knew what he was doing here. He felt nothing in himself of heroism and glory.

Only hard work, horror and dismay marked his day and more and more he closed himself off from feelings and emotions in order to be able to endure and persevere. The weeks passed slowly and the month of June began with very warm temperatures.

*

Aiden was now to be sent with a squad to Fort Vaux in Verdun, France, near the village of Vaux-Devant-Damloup, in mid-June, to join the French in repelling massive German attacks on the fort.
But things turned out differently, because on 7 June 1916, the troops under commander Sylvain Eugéne Raynal surrendered to the Germans and the counterattacks to defend the fort on the following days were unsuccessful.
And so it happened that the Germans were to occupy Fort Vaux until the end of October.
Therefore, in mid-June, the French gave the order to send the squad with the still very young, strong and fresh soldiers destined for Fort Vaux directly to the front at the Sommé.
Its mission was to support the 7-day artillery preparations from 24 June 1916 for the start of the Sommé battle between Gommécourt northwest of Bapaume and Vermandovillers southwest of Péronne. The start of the infantry attack was planned for 1 July 1916.
So they were split up partly by trains, partly by long marches, Aiden arrived with the troop in the French region of Hauts-de-France on the river Sommé in Flanders, in the west of France.

*

On arrival on 23 June 1916, Aiden was posted to the Irish 36th Division. What he could not yet know was that this Ulster Division, with which he was to fight on 1 July 1916, would lose over half its soldiers in this one battle alone.

This became the heaviest losing day in British military history. On that day alone, the British troops lost around 60,000 men, including around 20,000 killed in action.

In total, there were 104 divisions with 2.5 million soldiers in the Battle of the Sommé from July 1916 to November 1916. This first major combat mission became a traumatic event for Aiden. He later realised that he had probably only survived that day because his inexperience meant that he had been ordered, along with many other newcomers, not to leave the front line trench but to hold position there to eliminate any invading enemies.

Aiden did not know after hours how many shots he had fired and how many soldiers he had shot.

The trench was full of corpses and wounded. Germans, French and British united in death. For although the battlefields were very wide, soldiers from the enemy German camp kept advancing far and wide.

During breaks in the fighting, more trenches were dug and fortified, well into the night. Every day the neglect increased and the soldiers' strength diminished.

Every fortnight, they were replaced for a few days by other soldiers and taken to the front camp, which was located a short distance behind the front line, so that they could gather strength.

The weeks in July and August were marked by cruelty and suffering.

Aiden could hardly feel himself and, like most of the other soldiers, only functioned on command.

*

September had already arrived. For two days, Aiden had been sitting in the trenches with the other soldiers, or lying in their cramped and dirty dugouts, waiting for the next big attack.

The front lines were far apart. The men kept to themselves in the trenches. Reaching the German trenches would have been dangerous, as they were on the move with machine guns, firing from fixed positions and mowing down any advancing troops.

The soldiers were waiting for an order and thought that there might be a counterattack by the Germans, but this did not happen. So they had no desire to move further than necessary from their front trench. They lay tired in their sleeping bays or sat in the mud in the wider corridors of the trenches, since it had rained the days before, waiting for the next meal and the redeeming sleep.

But the next morning, the planned big battle was to begin. By order of the general, the fire would be opened.

At 6 o'clock on the morning of 6 September, the French General Joseph Joffre issued the order of the day:

"to the poor.... At a moment when a battle is taking place on which the fate of the country depends, it is important to remind everyone that this is not the moment to look backwards; every effort must be made to attack and repel the enemy. A force that makes no

further progress must, whatever the cost, hold the ground it has captured and allow itself to be killed in place rather than retreat. In the present circumstances, further hesitation cannot be tolerated." (Source Wikipedia "Battle of the Sommé)

*

Aiden hardly slept on this last night of the impending battle. He lay with his comrades in the dugout of the trench and stared up at the black sky.

Every now and then a mouse or a rat as big as rabbits scurried between their feet and he was afraid of being attacked by one of these giant rats.

He closed his eyes so as not to see those darting shadows any more. But sometimes he blinked, his eyes open a crack, at the sky. There he could make out individual stars in the black night sky, but they were always obscured by grey clouds. He had not seen his friend John, with whom he had left Ireland, for weeks.

He had been assigned to another unit.

Around Aiden, many Englishmen among his Irish compatriots. Many soldiers in his units had been fighting for some time and were jaded and apathetic. Most seemed cold and hardened. But many, like Aiden, had the sheer fear of the coming battle written all over their faces.

It was unusually quiet that night. Each of the soldiers was aware that in a few hours they would have to be ready and open fire.

Some took out their letters that they had received from their wives or families and read them again.

Looked at the pictures of their wives and children for a long time or showed them to their comrades. No one spoke up, some even slept. Nerves were on edge to such an extent that this had already led to rigidity or even insanity in many.

The soldiers who had already been on duty since the beginning of the war in 1914 were particularly affected. Again and again they alternated between two weeks in the trenches, then they were transferred to the stage for a few days. But these days passed too quickly and they had to return to the trenches and face an undignified existence and constant danger to their lives.

Many of the soldiers were only a functioning shell of themselves.

Usually, soldiers who served directly at the front were sent home after two years because they were so burnt out that they could no longer perform in combat. But the troops could no longer be replenished with enough fresh soldiers and therefore every man was needed, even if many hardly knew what they were doing anymore.

Aiden retreated in his mind in those hours before the battle to his own world, to Ireland, to a life that was poor but he had grown up in peace and in beautiful surroundings near the Hills of Tara.

The night passed and he watched and listened more and more to the silent orders moving through the trench.

Again and again, new observers were sent out to scout the enemy.

This was a very dangerous task that was only undertaken by experienced soldiers, as snipers and artillery observers from the enemy would sense any movement and immediately launch an attack.

As the morning slowly began to dawn, many of the soldiers became very restless.

Hardly anyone spoke a word as they shovelled their meagre breakfast, a bowl of porridge, into their mouths with a spoon and drank the thin broth infused with coffee substitute powder.

Aiden was already leaning against the trench wall, loading his rifle, again and again.

His hands were shaking with excitement and he was afraid that he would not manage to reload the cartridges.

A somewhat older soldier who came from London, his name was James, he told him, watched Aiden as he handled his rifle.

James shook his head as he examined the rifle.

There were different versions of the operational weapon. The Enfield rifle, whose standard equipment included a bayonet, could fire a maximum of 20 rounds in succession.

The rifle Aiden was holding was a version of one that was actually only used for training purposes and every single shot had to be reloaded.

He had received this rifle yesterday as a replacement, as there was a shortage of weapons of war.

James took the rifle from Aiden's hand.

"I'll get you another one. It's madness with this rifle that you have to reload after every shot."

James walked away and returned shortly afterwards with a new rifle that could fire twenty rounds in succession.

Aiden thanked him and took a closer look at the weapon.

"You will not be spared this time and must also go out onto the field. The order says that all men must fight on the battlefield beyond the trenches," the soldier informed him.

Aiden broke out in a sweat at the thought. But he knew he had no choice.

James gave him a few more tips and advised him to shoot only from the trench for as long as possible. He grasped his shoulder fatherly and wished him good luck.

The moment had come.

The commander hurriedly ran through the trench and gave the first signal for the attack. On the opposite German front, everything was still quiet, as the artillery observers had reported.

Some soldiers crept cautiously over the edge of the trench. Dusk had already set in, but it was not yet light. Not a cloud showed in the sky, so it would be a sunny day.

At dawn, the outlines of the counter-front could be seen in the distance.

Everything was still quiet. The lush green landscape between the fronts still seemed fairytale-like and calm for the moment.

Aiden stopped in the trench and no one took any notice of him. Every single person was busy with himself, waiting for the order to attack.

Then it was time.

He flinched as the first volleys of gunfire erupted. Everyone started running and a hellish noise began.

Aiden didn't know what was happening to him for the first few minutes. A hail of bullets everywhere.

Some soldiers who were particularly ready to fight charged up the makeshift wooden ladders, only to run and die in the vast vegetation, towards the opposite side.

He continued to hold back, thinking of James' words to stay

in the trench or near his own trench as long as possible to defend it from advancing enemies.

Great fear gripped Aiden and he was shocked to see the many dead already lying around him.

But then everyone was called to rush into open combat on the field in front of them and attack and push back the opponent.

Aiden tried to block out his fear. Suddenly he felt sick and had to throw up, but it was no use, he had to follow the other soldiers.

With trembling knees, he climbed up the wooden ladder, seeing the vast battlefield before him. Like an ant invasion, comrades were also climbing up the ladders next to him and running screaming.

Aiden's knees seemed to give way, only with difficulty did he hold on to the ladder. Then he grabbed his rifle, took hold of his bayonet, which was attached to the front of his belt, and charged off, shooting wildly, without a precise target. Again and again he fell, stumbling over wounded and already dead soldiers.

He didn't know how long he had been running, was it minutes or hours, when he stumbled and just lay there. His face was in the mud and he could only breathe a little.

He did not move. He didn't look left or right, just lay motionless. Frozen in fear and terror, he thought to himself to simply close his eyes and not get up again.

Suddenly he was grabbed under the shoulder and dragged up.

Aiden let it happen and expected to be shot immediately. But he was dragged along by the strong arms.

He didn't know where to go until he was laid down on the edge of the trench.

"Are you hurt? Jump back in the trench boy, quick!" the soldier who had dragged him here shouted at him. It was James who kept shouting at him.

Aiden didn't move, just lay there and stared at the man, who then gave him a shove with his foot and he fell into the trench with full force unchecked.

When he hit the bottom, he cried out and woke up as if from a trance.

He awoke from his rigidity and slowly saw and thought clearly again. He struggled to pull himself up. Completely exhausted, he leaned against the trench wall. Powerless, he sank to his knees and dropped his rifle. He hated weapons and hated this war even more.

For a brief moment he closed his eyes.

He was so tired and didn't know how long he had to hold out, how long the fight would last. There was complete chaos around him.

His comrades were either running around uncontrollably or lying injured, moaning loudly at the foot of the trench, waiting for help. In between lay the dead.

He blanked out the cruel happenings around him. He only wanted to rest for a short moment. Powerlessly, he raised his trembling hands.

He already couldn't remember what it was like not to shiver. He thought of how the sky had still been blue yesterday morning. And he saw this sky in front of him, the black clouds of smoke from the guns, tanks and cannons had vanished in his imagination, no sounds could be heard, no gunshots, no cries of the wounded or dying.

He looked up at the sky, closed his eyes and for a brief moment he breathed in the cool, fresh air of memory, transporting himself for moments back to his homeland in Ireland. He saw the green, lush meadows, the old oak tree, high up on the hill, near his childhood home. He thought of the old, huge, green-covered hilltop burial ground, New Grange, which he could see in the distance from there. He loved his native Ireland more than anything.

He thought of his parents, of his sister Eimear and of the fact that he would probably never see them again. This war was so cruel and yet there was no escape.

*

Still leaning with his back against the wall of the trench, with trembling hands and tears in his eyes, Aiden thought of his parents and the day he had left them.

If only he had had an inkling that this was a journey of no return, he would have made a different decision.

But today, almost six months later, he was here in the trenches in France, in the midst of a cruel battle, surrounded by the wounded and the dead. Today, 6 September, was his birthday. He turned 19 years old.

His birthday was spent in this cruel battle and he feared that his birthday would also be the day of his death.

Automatically, Aiden grabbed the pocket of his grey, dirty uniform trousers. Thank God, it was still there. Through the fabric of the trousers, he could feel the outline of the coin.

"Please help me," Aiden whispered desperately, "I don't want to die."

Tears streamed down his face while a soldier fell down the trench next to him and lay bleeding. Aiden bent down to him.

The man grabbed his hand and held on to him. Aiden looked around frantically and began to shout loudly for the paramedics. But no one heard him.

The air was too permeated with rifle shots, cannon blasts and the screams of soldiers on the battlefield and in the trenches.

He bent towards the man again, but he had closed his eyes and his hand went limp.

Aiden's hand was still shaking. His gaze wandered wildly. He knew he had to get back to the field. He couldn't stay down here and wait until it was all over.

He knew that even if he survived this fight, which was unlikely given the scale of it, the next fight would come and it would start all over again.

No, Aiden had no choice.

One last time he closed his eyes briefly, thought of his parents and his sister and quickly said a prayer.

Christ with me,
Christ before me,
Christ behind me,
Christ within me,
Christ below me,
Christ above me,.
Christ on my right hand,
Christ on my left hand,
Christ on my sleeping,
Christ in my waking,

Christ in the heart of all who
think of me,
Christ in the mouth of all
who speak of me,
Christ in every eye that
looks at me,
Christ in every ear
that listens to me.
(St. Patrick's Breastplate)

This prayer gave him strength. Every Sunday he went to church with his parents.

He never took it seriously and often did not understand why people were so attached to these prayers. Now he could understand it. It gave him support in these situations and it had been with him all the last months he spent here in the war.

Aiden could understand how important it was to have something to believe in when hardship, fear and death were at the door.

He struggled to pull himself up. The arm of the dead soldier next to him fell from his lap onto the muddy earth. Aiden bent down again and put both hands on the soldier's stomach and crossed himself.

Then he took his rifle, went towards the nearest ladder and climbed up.

He wanted to face the battle and death, for he had no choice. He took a deep breath as he looked at the vast battlefield in front of him and ran.

*

Aiden ran like a madman. He screamed so loudly that his lungs hurt. He ran across the battlefield, through the already badly damaged vegetation, towards the enemy. He could see little, for the air was grey and murky from the smoke of the cannon shots and tank attacks.

The whole battlefield partly resembled a burnt and charred plain. Scorched grass on scorched earth, scattered charred tree stumps. Injured or dead bodies lay everywhere, and he stumbled over them. Shots whizzed past his head and body. But he hardly noticed them and kept running. He cried out with tears running down his cheeks.

Not once had he fired, although he held his rifle at the ready. Suddenly he felt a pain in his legs. He had run into a barbed wire barrier that had already been half trampled down and was used by the other side, i.e. Germany, to secure their position. He had already run too close to the German front line.

Aiden had to stop, otherwise he would have fallen with his whole body into the barbed wire.

With his bare hands and screaming even louder, he tried to free himself from the fence undergrowth. Adrenalin pumped through his body like a drug.

At last he had managed to free himself. Impatiently, he tore at his legs. His hands were bloody, as were his legs under the now finally torn trousers.

Aiden didn't care. He no longer felt any pain, as if he had cut off all feeling.

When he had finally broken free, he rushed on blindly to the left. He had left his rifle behind.

All this happened within minutes, during which his thinking was completely switched off.

Suddenly he stopped, the chaos raging on. Not far from Aiden, a cannonball struck. Rocks and earth pelted him.

He heard the screams of soldiers who had been hit.

As if in a trance, he kept running after grabbing a rifle that was lying on the ground next to him. He looked back briefly and suddenly felt a sharp pain in his right leg and went down on his knees. He quickly pulled himself up again.

But a shot had hit his right leg and literally torn it open, below the knee.

Aiden ran a few more steps, then stumbled and fell into a funnel created by a tank shell.

There it fell directly on a soldier lying at the foot of the crater, who let out a bloodcurdling cry of pain.

Startled, Aiden immediately wanted to stand up, but the hand of the soldier lying under him held him back.

The man grabbed him by his jacket and pulled him firmly onto his body. Now the two were lying face to face.

Aiden stared fearfully at the man as he suddenly realised the pain in his leg and began to moan loudly.

Meanwhile, he recognised from the soldier's field-grey uniform that he was a German soldier.

An icy shock ran through Aiden.

The man moved his lips as if he wanted to tell him something, but Aiden could not understand him.

After only a moment's hesitation, he put his ear to his mouth. The soldier began to move his lips again.

"Lie still, boy. I won't hurt you," the soldier whispered in pain and a language Aiden couldn't understand.

Aiden did not understand a word. What was the soldier trying to tell him? He looked irritatedly into the soldier's red eyes, which were full of pain and widened in fear.

"Stay boy. Do not be afraid of me," the soldier struggled to say in English.

Aiden looked at him in surprise.

The German soldier spoke English to him.

"You speak my language?" Still amazed, he looked him in the face.

Suddenly, machine gun shots whizzed over Aiden's head away. He quickly rolled off the German soldier's body and lay pressed against him on the ground beside him. The hail of bullets stopped and Aiden raised his head again.

The German soldier turned to face him. Aiden saw that the left side of his stomach was bleeding profusely under the German soldier's torn, field-grey tunic.

When he turned back to the German soldier's face, he saw that his gaze was dull with pain. And Aiden, too, could hardly stand the pain on his leg and groaned loudly with every wave of pain.

He did not know what to do. Again the soldier grabbed him by his uniform jacket and pulled him close.

"My father was a German diplomat who knew the English language. That's why I understand your language," the soldier whispered to him. "What is your name? How old are you boy?"

"Aiden, my name is Aiden. I'm nineteen years old," he replied. "It's my birthday today," tears came to his eyes.

The situation was completely surreal for Aiden.

The German soldier suddenly groaned loudly and held his hand to his injured left side.

"Happy birthday, my boy," he pressed out strainedly, trying to smile.

"What's your name?", Aiden asked the man.

"Franz, my name is Franz von Letten and I am 41 years old, my boy. You could be my son. Where are you from?"

"From Ireland," Aiden replied.

Slowly he began to trust the German soldier.

He simply remained lying next to him. Around them, the chaos of war reigned.

"Ireland," the soldier repeated. "My father was already there and told me about the green country when I was a child."

For a moment Franz looked up at the smoke-drenched sky above him.

"I'm going to die my boy."

Aiden grabbed Franz by his right sleeve and shook him.

"No, Franz, we are not going to die. The battle will soon be over and the medics will save us," Aiden yelled helplessly and desperately.

Within that short time, Aiden immediately felt a strong bond with this German soldier in the midst of this cruelty.

Even though they were both enemies, he felt that this German felt no hatred towards him, just as he felt no hostility.

"Are you badly hurt?" asked Franz, raising his head a little.

"I got hit in the leg."

"Are you missing anything else?", Franz weakly put his hand on Aiden's arm.

"No, I don't think so," Aiden replied.

"That's good. I'll make you a proposal now. And we must act quickly, my boy. You shall survive this war."

Just minutes ago, Aiden saw himself at the mercy of certain death as he ran onto the battlefield.

But now, at Franz's words, he suddenly felt a rebellion inside him. He wanted to live, he didn't want to die.

"We will survive the war. Both of us, you and me," Aiden cried out desperately.

"Listen to me, boy. We're swapping uniforms. Or rather, what's left of them."

Startled, Aiden looked at Franz.

"Why should we change uniforms? Why?"

"Because you're too close to the German front line. Why did you walk so close to the German trench in the first place? When they collect the wounded after the battle, they will hold you as a prisoner of war or, at worst, shoot you right here on the spot, as is so often done by many a battle-hardened soldier," Franz spoke urgently to Aiden. "Do you want to end up in a mass grave here on your birthday?"

Tears came to Aiden's eyes again, from fear and also from the pain in his leg.

An unbelievable panic spread in his head.

He could not think clearly and only wanted to close his eyes and wake up from this nightmare.

"But how is that going to work?", Aiden looked at Franz in irritation.

"You have to help me. I can hardly move. You have to take off my shoes, trousers and jacket, even if it's pretty tattered and bloody. I'm sorry," Franz whispered.

Speaking was incredibly tiring for him.

"Then you put your clothes on me. I'm already so emaciated that the size shouldn't be a problem.

And the length of your trouser legs is no longer noticeable, as tattered as your trousers are."

Aiden stared at Franz in disbelief.

"Don't think long, boy. Just listen to me. You have no choice. Do what I tell you.

It's getting a little quieter already. We don't have long to explain.

We'll swap uniforms, you'll be taken by the Germans to a military hospital and, if you're lucky, sent home if you're not fit for war with your leg for the time being."

"Home? But I'm home in Ireland!" cried Aiden bitterly.

"Kid, you don't have another chance. Please pull yourself together. We have to hurry," Franz affirmed once again in a brittle voice, straining to recall the English words.

"How is that supposed to work? I don't know the German language? I don't know anyone in Germany. I am an enemy. And where am I supposed to go in Germany?" cried Aiden desperately, his voice drenched in fear.

"No, my boy, we are not enemies. The men fighting here are not enemies. They have been made enemies by the supposedly powerful in their country," Franz whispered bitterly before continuing to press Aiden.

"Good, the language will be a problem, of course. You won't speak a word until you master the German language. That won't be very noticeable, because many traumatised soldiers don't speak or hear anything anymore. You have to be clever, then you'll manage. My wife will help you. And when the war is over, you can go back to your home country."

Aiden was still listening to Franz in disbelief. The plan he was proposing was outrageous and he felt totally overwhelmed.

"Go to my wife. Tell her about me, about our meeting",

Tears were now streaming down Franz's cheeks as he thought of his wife Elisabeth.

"Tell her how we met. Tell her how much I love her and that I will watch over her from heaven.

And tell her that I know she will take good care of you and help you. My boy, she will, I'm sure she will. She is a good woman, with a big heart. And she has always wanted a boy, which unfortunately was not granted to us. Elisabeth, my wife, can also speak a little English, you will understand each other.

Exhausted by the pain and his explanations, Franz closed his eyes.

Aiden's head was pounding.

What should he do? Should he accept the proposal that this German soldier was offering him?

Maybe this really gave him a chance to break out of this war he so rashly and naively manoeuvred himself into? But will he be able to endure all this?

The prospect of surviving and then one day returning to his family after the war suddenly put all his concerns in the background. But he also did not want Franz, the German soldier, to die.

"Boy, come on. Don't think so long. I can't hold out much longer. Hurry up. This is your chance."

Aiden straightened up a little.

The pain in his foot was hellish and his flesh was burning up to his thigh. In tears, he began to take off his jacket. They were well protected by the depression of the crater.

The gunfire around them had become less. Too many soldiers had already fallen in this battle.

Dark clouds of smoke hovered over the battlefield and did not allow for a wide view. You could hardly see your hand in front of your eyes. But this circumstance was very helpful to Aiden and Franz.

When Aiden slipped his trousers off his legs after untying and removing his shoes, he cried out in pain. He pressed his mouth against his jacket sleeve and bit his own arm to keep from screaming even louder.

Franz watched him do this and with his right hand he unbuttoned his single-breasted uniform jacket in the meantime.

He then tore off the detachable epaulettes from the jacket, which had piping indicating the army corps in which he served. Likewise, the regimental number and his monogram were embroidered on the flaps themselves.

Franz tore the flaps from his shoulders and threw them as far as he could. Aiden should not be able to be assigned to his regiment, because otherwise someone would have to be who knew him, Franz, would be suspicious.

Franz had a plan in his head within minutes. He wanted to save this boy.

He felt that he was going to die. He had been hurt too badly. His strength was fading by the minute and Franz hoped he could hold out until Aiden had dressed him to some extent. Franz wanted his death to have at least one meaning, that a boy like Aiden might survive.

Franz would have helped anyone else too.

He was a teacher at a boys' school in Germany, in Munich, and was very socially minded from an early age.

Only a few days ago, he had received a letter from his wife saying that the school had been turned into a military hospital because of a lack of space in the existing hospitals.

She wrote to him that the children were taught in the basement of the houses in a makeshift way.

But most parents had sent their children to the countryside because they were safer there.

Elisabeth also wrote him how much she missed him and was afraid for him. And she wrote that he should hang in there and take care of himself. That she hugged him and was looking forward to picking him up from the train soon, when he returned from this fruitful war.

Yes, his Elisabeth firmly believed that they would meet again.

Tears ran down Franz's cheeks at the memories of the letter and of his wife.

He thought of his school, which no longer existed, just as he would soon no longer exist in this world. Everything was destroyed by this senseless war, cities, villages, houses, streets, entire landscapes. Human lives were sacrificed for power and greed. There was no escaping this power of command.

*

By now Aiden was sweating so much from exertion that water was running down his face.

But before he took off his long johns, he helped Franz with the difficult task of taking off his trousers. Blood was all over his jacket and trousers. Due to Franz's abdominal injury, it was difficult to get him out of his clothes. Every movement caused him indescribable pain and he could hardly stand up by himself.

Aiden had to support him on his back so that he could pull the jacket off his arms. Franz groaned loudly again and again. When it was finally done, it was the turn of his trousers.

As Aiden undid the buttons of his trousers, tears came to his eyes again at the sight of the deep abdominal wound.

The cotton vest was blood-soaked and torn at this point. Underneath, Aiden saw more and more blood running from the wound.

He quickly took a scarf from the inside pocket of his uniform jacket, in which he had wrapped the golden coin just before the fight. He quickly took the coin out and placed it in his shoe, which was standing to the side of him, so that it could not get lost in the hustle and bustle of clothing.

Then he pressed the scarf onto the wound to stop the bleeding. Franz groaned loudly.

"Franz, please hold your hand on this."

When Franz only responded with another pained sound, Aiden grabbed his right hand and placed it on the scarf.

"Here, hold the cloth and press it on the wound," Aiden repeated desperately.

"I'm trying to get your pants off now."

Aiden groaned loudly as he pulled on his trousers and Franz's eyes widened in pain, an inhuman sound escaping his mouth.

*

All this happened in the midst of the battle that was still raging around the two men. The clouds of smoke grew thicker and suddenly Aiden was thrown onto Franz by a violent blow he received on his back. Franz cried out loudly and Aiden tried to get up quickly.

But this undertaking was not so easy, as he felt massive weight on his back.

And only now did he realise that a soldier was lying behind him, on his back.

With all his strength Aiden straightened up and turned around and the dead soldier slid to the ground.

"Feel if he still has a pulse," Franz whispered exhaustedly.

Aiden quickly grabbed the man's neck with his fingers, but he could no longer feel a pulse.

It was also a soldier wearing a British uniform.

For a few seconds Aiden closed his eyes and would have liked to just lie down on the ground, never to get up again.

"Come on boy. Get up. We have to keep going. We don't have much time left," Franz called out in a mat voice.

Aiden straightened up and they looked into each other's eyes for seconds.

Franz's clouded gaze, in which pain was evident, begged Aiden for courage.

Come on boy, they seemed to say, and he mustered the last of his strength.

He rolled the dead soldier a few inches away from him before turning back to Franz.

He quickly unlaced Franz's shoes and slipped them off his feet. Then he pulled his trousers off his legs. Then, with great difficulty, he removed his long grey pants.

Immediately afterwards he took his own tattered pants and pulled them up over Franz's legs. And also the bloody uniform trousers, whose right leg consisted only of shreds from the knee down.

Aiden managed all this in an inhuman posture and effort. Half sitting, half lying, sweating, crying and screaming, because he could not kneel with his leg.

He quickly pulled Franz's grey, woollen pants over his healthy leg before tearing the second leg open with all his might up to his knee and pulling it over his injured leg, groaning in pain. Lying down, he pulled the pants up.

Then Aiden supported Franz as he tried to take off his vest. But Franz cried out in pain and Aiden let him sink back.

He tried another way. He rolled Franz's vest up to his chest, pulled first his left arm, then his right arm out of his sleeves, and finally pulled the vest over his head. At last it was done. Exhausted, Aiden let himself sink back onto his back.

When he lifted his gaze again, he saw that Franz was keeping his eyes closed.

"Franz, Franz!" cried Aiden in panic and bent over his face. But Franz did not react. Was he dead?

*

Again and again he grabbed Franz by the shoulders and shook him desperately, in tears.

"Franz, Franz, please, you must not die!"

Despondent, Aiden let himself fall back. What was he to do now? Franz lay half-dressed in front of him. He couldn't leave him lying like that.

He searched for his own vest among the throng of clothes. Then he pulled it over Franz's head and carefully tucked his arms into the sleeves, pulling it as gently as he could over his wounded, bleeding belly.

The bloody scarf had slipped from the wound and was lying on the floor next to Franz. Aiden lifted it up and pressed it back onto the still bleeding wound on his stomach.

At that moment he heard a soft moan and he saw that Franz's eyelids began to flutter. He quickly bent over his face.

"Franz, Franz, can you hear me?" he shouted again desperately. Aiden could hardly hear his own voice because several bombs were hitting nearby again.

Then finally, Franz opened his eyelids a little. Dazed and surprised, he looked at Aiden, but then he began to understand where he was and realised again his pain, which made him groan. He took a few deep breaths and closed his eyes again. But then he moved his lips and strained to form words with his mouth.

"Son, in my jacket pocket is the letter for my wife. Please take it to her. Tell her that I'm sorry I can't go back to her and that I love her very much," he whispered in a weak voice. Aiden could barely hear him, so he held his ear very close to Franz's mouth.

"Yes Franz, I will tell her, for sure I will find her," Aiden replied desperately.

Franz lifted his arm and gently stroked Aiden's pain-ravaged face with his hand and a grateful smile appeared on his parched lips.

"You know what you have to do now, boy. The address in Munich is on the letter. I wish you all the best.
You will find a way. Believe in it."

These last words were barely audible and Franz closed his eyes and his breath faltered a few times before it went out completely, his arm fell powerlessly to the ground and his head tilted to the side.

Aiden sat next to Franz in a daze. Now he was all alone again. The pain inside him seemed to overwhelm him, drowning out the pain in his leg so that he could hardly breathe.

He sat motionless for a moment. A tremendous heaviness settled on his soul. What should he do now?

For a few seconds he thought about just giving up. Just throwing himself onto the battlefield and into the hail of bullets and surrendering to his fate. But then he thought of his family back home in Ireland. And an immense strength in him at the thought made him take a deep breath all at once.

He raised his head, looked at Franz, then turned to the dead soldier lying behind him and suddenly knew with an inner certainty that he wanted to live. Yes, he chose to live in that small moment of strength within him.

Whether he would make it out of this war was another matter, but he, Aiden McGilles, decided to at least try.

Franz offered him this chance to slip into the role of a German soldier, to get a little chance.

And if he played his part well, maybe one day he would see his family again in Ireland.

Aiden reached to his shoes and took out the golden coin from one of the shoes and held it in tears
in his hands.

What had the goblin said to him then about the power of the coin?

She would help him in any hopeless situation. And she had sent him, Aiden, to Franz. And now Franz had offered him this opportunity, this miracle.

Quickly he put the coin back into the shoe. And with this power and strength flooding his body and senses, he put on

47

Franz's uniform, which was covered all over with blood, dirt and dust.

He tore open the right trouser leg, which he had pulled over his wounded leg in pain, and shredded it as best he could, just as he had done earlier with the woollen pants, so that his injured leg lay open.

When he had finished dressing, he reached into his shoe and took out the golden coin and slipped it into the inside pocket of his grey uniform jacket. As he did so, he felt for the letter Franz had spoken of, the one he had written to his wife Elisabeth in case he didn't make it home.

Aiden pulled it out carefully. He did not want to damage it in any way.

On the outside was the address in Germany. And he knew that would be his point of contact in Germany. The letter was addressed to Elisabeth von Letten, living at Agnesstraße 11 in Munich, Germany, he deciphered the foreign German words.

Aiden held the letter close to his heart for a moment. What would Franz's wife say if he suddenly appeared at her place? How will she react when she learns of her husband's death and he, a stranger, appears at her door? Will she really take him in and help him?

He immediately shooed away these thoughts, because first he had to make it there in the first place.

Aiden realised he would be dependent on her. For just one careless word out of his mouth could ruin the whole plan, he was very aware of that.

He put the letter back into the inside pocket of the uniform jacket. Then he closed the remaining buttons of the jacket. Once again he bent over Franz.

"I will take the letter to your wife and tell her about your last words. I promise you."

Then he took his own uniform jacket and pulled it over Franz's right arm.

With all his strength, he then lifted Franz's upper body a little and pushed the jacket behind his back. When he tried to get Franz's left arm into the sleeve of the jacket, he saw that it was hopeless. The jacket was simply too small for Franz and he didn't want to break his arm. Even if he would no longer feel it. So he left it under his back. He knew that no one would pay any attention to it. Finally, he pulled his boots over his feet.

Aiden wondered what he should do now. Just stay here? Protected in this bomb hole next to the two corpses? He listened up.

He did not know how much time had passed. There were only isolated gun salvos and bombs were falling at long intervals. But Aiden was aware that it could go on for days. This was only a brief respite before the battle would continue.

Above the bomb crater where Aiden was, a thin veil of smoke drifted across the field. Again and again he heard scattered bursts from machine guns in the distance.

Aiden half straightened and peered over the edge of the bomb crater.

Dead soldiers lay everywhere. The ground was burnt and resembled a devastated stone field. A cemetery for thousands of men who were prepared to sacrifice their lives. Who, voluntarily or involuntarily, had gone to this war to fight for their fatherland and hoped they would come home healthy to their families as heroes.

And now they lay here, dead, senselessly fought and died for power, heroism and possessions that no one could take with them into death.

Aiden bent back into the bomb crater. Again he wondered what to do? Wait here?

He lay on his back and stared up at the smoke-drenched sky in the middle of no man's land between the fronts.

Suddenly an incredible exhaustion overcame him and his eyelids began to flutter and he sank into a deep swoon.

*

Aiden opened his eyes with difficulty. It took him a moment to realise where he was. But in seconds he realised what had happened. He sat up frantically and instantly felt nauseous and nothing but bile shot out of his mouth. He wiped his face with his sleeve and looked at Franz, who lay pale and frozen beside him. Aiden did not know how long he had been lying there.

The air was still clouded by the smoke. His mouth was parched and his lips torn and bloody. Slowly and with a tremendous effort, he pushed his body up with his arms and turned onto his stomach. With his healthy leg he supported himself against the crater wall and heaved himself up a little. Cautiously, he peered over the edge of the crater.

Aiden bent back into the bomb crater. Again he wondered what to do? Wait here?

Suddenly he perceived a demonic silence that lay over the battlefield.

He held his breath and peered cautiously over the edge of his protective crater again.

Everything was quiet, eerily quiet, until suddenly scattered moans of the wounded could be heard, growing louder and louder.

It took a while for everyone to wake up from their state of shock and also to hear this silence, and then all at once to emit timid cries for help, as far as they could still make a sound.

Aiden's gaze fell to Franz one last time before he crawled out of the bomb crater.

With his arms he pulled himself up and as best he could, he helped with his healthy left leg.

He could not move his right leg.

It hurt like hell. In the last few minutes he had hardly noticed this pain. The adrenaline pumped non-stop through his body, helping him to block out the pain and hang on.

When he was at the top, at the edge of the bomb crater, he crawled further and further forward. He wanted to be a good distance away from Franz so that they wouldn't be connected in any way.

Briefly he considered whether he might manage to crawl back into his own trench. But when he looked down at himself, he realised that he was now wearing Franz's German uniform. He also knew that he was too far away. He quickly dismissed this thought and crawled on with difficulty.

When he had made it a few metres, past countless dead and wounded, whimpering bodies, he lay exhausted on his stomach and closed his eyes. He was at the end of his tether and let go of any struggle within him, whereupon he fell into a relieving unconsciousness.

*

51

Aiden opened his eyes. He was still lying prone on the battlefield. He covered his face with one arm. He woke from his unconsciousness and wondered, dazed, how long he had been lying there like that.

He raised his head. There was a demonic atmosphere.

No sounds of battle, no cannon blasts could be heard at the moment. Everything seemed to stand still. Only the desperate groans and inhuman cries of injured soldiers pierced the silence.

Clouds of smoke still lay over the battlefield.

The battle stood still for a moment. The monster devoured its prey.

Only dimly could Aiden make out the soldiers lying scattered around him. Many injured, many dead.

Not far from him, he saw a figure that kept trying to get up, but failed each time. Both legs were torn off.

Aiden averted his eyes. An indescribable feeling of horror ran through his body and suddenly he was aware of the pain in his leg again.

Like a wave it rolled over him and he sank his face into his hands with a loud groan.

After a few minutes, he rolled onto his back and looked up at the grey sky above him. Tears streamed down his face and he whimpered like a little child.

"Mum, Dad, where are you!" he whispered in despair, "I wish I had never left you."

Suddenly he heard loud shouts and turned his head to the side.

"Always two men together. Turn each one over and see if they are still alive. Take the wounded with you, leave the

52

dead, we'll get them later. And take the English and the French with you. Hurry up. «

Through the clouds of smoke, he saw completely exhausted but unharmed soldiers streaming onto the battlefield.

Aiden watched three men running towards him. He began to shake all over and closed his eyes, overcome by fear and pain in his leg.

The men were now standing in front of him and he heard one of them say something and then poke him in the side with his foot. Aiden groaned loudly as the pain coursed through his whole body.

"Hey you, are you still alive?" one of the men shouted crudely.

Aiden kept quiet out of fear, not understanding a word.

"He must have lost his tongue," said another of the men, kneeling down to him and roughly patting his cheek.

Aiden opened his eyes and looked directly into the face of one of the German soldiers who was leaning close over his face.

"He's still alive!" he shouted and made a hand gesture towards the stretcher.

"Put him on the stretcher right away and take him to the dressing area."

"What is your name?" asked the man kneeling in front of him.

Panic continued in Aiden. He did not understand the man. What was he supposed to do? How should he behave?

What a stupid idea, he thought, to pretend to be a German soldier.

He would be exposed in no time and then end up as a prisoner of war or perhaps shot right here. He didn't know which would be the better choice.

Suddenly, the man kneeling in front of him grabbed the inside of his uniform jacket.

"If you're not going to say anything, at least give me your badge," the soldier shouted impatiently. He continued to search the inside pocket of the jacket.

He finally pulled out the letter that was intended for Elisabeth, Franz's wife.

On the envelope was her name 'Elisabeth von Letten' and the address 'Agnesstraße 11 in Munich'.

"Ah, there we have something already. Are you the Lord of Letten?". He looked scrutinisingly at Aiden. "Look, a Lord von und zu, then!" he called to the other two soldiers with a sneer.

Aiden was still silent. What could he say. He understood nothing, could say nothing, and so he just nodded his head.

Again a wave of pain overtook him, taking his breath away, and he closed his eyes, whimpering.

The soldier rose and left the other two men with the stretcher to join Aiden.

They grabbed him under the shoulders and by the leg that was not injured and dragged him roughly onto the stretcher. Aiden cried out loudly in pain and his eyes went black.

The soldiers put the letter back into the inside pocket of his uniform.

Briefly, the soldier looked for the dog tag, but he did not find the small leather case in which the dog tags were normally kept.

However, he had not discovered the golden coin in the small inside pocket of the uniform jacket.

He quickly put his fingers to the aorta of the unconscious Aiden's neck to feel whether he was only unconscious or had died. But he could clearly feel his pulse.

"Take him to the first aid station and then come back with the next stretcher," he ordered the other two soldiers and looked around to see which of the men lying on the ground was still moving.

*

West Front/France September 1916

Field hospital

"What's hitting me? No, leave me alone. I don't want to," it screamed inside Aiden and he flailed his hands around until he was held down by strong arms and he woke up from the nightmare.

Startled, he looked into the eyes of a tall man who leaned over him and held him by the arms. Aiden whispered silently to himself.

"Where am I?"

But at the last moment he was able to swallow the words into an indistinct murmur, because he remembered in a flash where and why he was here.

The man, whose dirty smock had certainly once been white, looked at him questioningly.

Aiden quickly closed his eyes again and let his head fall onto his side. He pretended to be unconscious.

He needed time to become clear and to think.

The doctor grabbed his forehead, then stood up, shouted something to someone else and moved away from the makeshift hospital bed, an unstable, narrow couch.

Aiden breathed a sigh of relief.

Then he was relieved to see that the pain in his leg had become a little more bearable.

Cautiously, he lifted his head, opened his eyes just a crack and looked down at himself.

Only a grey woollen blanket lay on his body, from which his bandaged leg protruded. Then he looked around.

He lay with several other injured people in a large grey tent with a large red cross painted in the fabric on the walls. Only a narrow corridor separated the injured from each other.

Most of the others lay asleep on the sickbeds. Others stared apathetically at the tent ceiling with their eyes open.

On his left side, a man with a thick bandage around his head and eyes lay moaning to himself.

Aiden put his head back again and closed his eyes. He couldn't think straight and felt foggy.

Again and again he thought what would happen next. He was at the mercy of the Germans, with the one advantage for him that they thought he was a German. But for how long? Would they transport him to Germany? Aiden didn't know if his injury was severe enough. Maybe they would take care of him here and then send him back to the front.

At the thought, a renewed panic overtook him. No, he would rather die right away than return to this cruel hell of a battle. But did he have a choice?

A young man, also in a very dirty, once probably white, smock, came to his bedside.

Aiden's eyes widened in fear when he saw the thing in the man's hands.

A long needle protruded from a round container that held a liquid. He had never seen anything like it before. He had never been to a doctor before either.

His mother had nursed him back to health with medicinal herbs and tea when he had a cold. And he has not had any serious illness so far. And besides, they couldn't have afforded a visit to the doctor.

*

His father was once in a hospital in Dublin after collapsing in the field. What he had missed, Aiden did not know. His father did not talk about his stay in hospital. Aiden was only 8 years old at the time and his mother took his father to Dublin on the hay cart with the harnessed horse. Neither returned for days. He and his sister Eimear, who was 12 at the time, stayed alone in the cottage during this time, looking after the chickens and sheep as best they could. Aiden often asked his sister about his parents and when they would be back. But Eimear could not give him an answer. She herself was very afraid that her parents would not come back.

But after a week, he was feeding the chickens next to the cottage when he heard a horse neighing and he looked up. Then he spotted his parents' hay cart and he ran towards them cheering after throwing the tin bowl with the grains on the ground.

*

Aiden's face broke into a smile as he thought of this event and felt the joy and relief he had felt when his parents had returned.

He thought wistfully of his parents, his sister and his home, there at the foot of the Hill of Tara, the fairy hills as they were also called in Ireland.

*

If you stand on the Hill of Tara, you can overlook a huge area there, in all directions. And in good, clear weather, you can see the mountains of all four Irish provinces - Munster, Leinster, Connacht and Ulster - from there. For centuries, the hill had been considered the home of gods and druids. His mother had often told him these legends and stories.

Aiden's favourite thing was to sit there, on a bench under a tree, and replay the stories that had once taken place here. And his favourite story was the one about the Lia Fáil stone, also called the Stone of Destiny, which stood at the top of the hill, now a landmark.

Once, High King Conn had been worried that his kingdom would be attacked from the universe. For this reason, he had druids and historians come to Tara and observe the starry sky closely.

During a speech, he is said to have stepped on a stone, which then screamed so loudly that it could be heard for miles. The stone was named Lia Fáil, Stone of Destiny. It is said that it still cries out today when Ireland is in danger.

*

Aiden awoke abruptly from his memories when he felt a hand on his arm.

Then his gaze fell again on this thing in the young doctor's hand. What did he want with it?

The man leaned down to him and said something. He looked at him with wide, suspicious eyes. The man said to him in German.

"I'm going to give you another injection now. This is penicillin.

59

You need this so that you don't get an infection in your leg. If that happens, we may have to amputate your leg after all. Do you understand me?" the young assistant doctor looked questioningly at Aiden when he noticed his confused look.

Aiden stared at the syringe, then back at the young doctor, not understanding a word.

Finally, he put both arms over his eyes in panic and groaned loudly.

"Do you understand me? I need your arm to give you the shot," the doctor said and grabbed Aiden's right arm.

But he resisted and crossed both arms firmly over his face.

Again the young doctor tried to pull his arm away from Aiden's face. But Aiden used all his strength to fight back.

The young doctor looked around helplessly. Already the older doctor came back to his bed.

"Well what's up Alois?"

"He won't let me give him the shot," he explained helplessly to his superior.

"We'll have that in a moment," said the doctor, standing behind Aiden, at the head of the couch, taking his arms from his face with all his strength and pressing them to the left and right of the couch, next to his body, holding him ironically. Aiden wanted to fight back, but he could not resist the doctor's steely grip. Then, as he struggled with his whole body, he cried out in pain as the jerky movement in his hip caused his legs to move as well. And a cruel pain shot through his injured leg, which immediately put him out of action.

He whimpered, surrendered and held still.

The doctor was talking to him. Aiden looked at him agitatedly.

"Boy, we have to give you the shot so you can keep your leg. Do you understand. Your leg will have to be cut off or you will die."

Aiden felt despair rising within him.

He did not understand a word. He could only guess what the doctor was trying to tell him by the gestures he made with his hand. He thought they wanted to prick him with this needle and then cut off his leg.

Still the doctor held his arms.

Aiden finally gave up and the doctor nodded to the young doctor who could now give him the injection.

Aiden watched him tap the crook of his arm and then drill the large needle into his flesh, making him cry out, partly in fright, partly in pain.

Instinctively, he wanted to fight back and moved his body again to defend himself, but the pain in his leg made him stop again immediately.

The pain, the anger and his fear made him let out a loud scream that came deep from his throat.

*

When he opened his eyes, he looked around in confusion. Where was he? Irritated and his senses as if trapped in a thick fog, he looked around until suddenly the memory came back to him. His leg, they were going to cut it off, he thought in panic and lifted his head to look down at himself.

Relieved, he saw that his leg was still there. But right now he felt no pain. What he did not know was that he was being treated with morphine. This opiate took away his pain, anxiety and mental and physical stress.

61

Aiden straightened up a little and looked around.

To his right lay a man whose face was almost completely bandaged. Only a narrow slit left his mouth free, through which a perpetual moan escaped.

To his left lay a soldier with only a short stump left of his left arm.

The soldier looked at him, but with a blank stare and silent. Aiden had the impulse to say something to him, but just then he held back.

Quickly he turned his head away, lay back on the hospital couch and tried to think.

It was not easy for him to organise his thoughts, as he could not grasp a clear thought through this fog in his head.

What would happen to him now?

He asked himself this question again and again. Would his leg perhaps not be so badly injured that they would send him back to the battlefield?

He groaned at the thought.

No, he doesn't want to go back to that cruelty.

Suddenly a tremendous thought came to him.

If it were the case that his leg would get better and he would have to go back to the battlefield, then he would fight on the wrong side.

Through this whole endeavour, he would be forced to shoot at his countrymen and fight against his country.

He crossed his arms in front of his face to hold back his tears. My God, how messed up the whole situation was. What should he do if it came to that?

For a while longer, he wrestled with his fears before he finally fell back into a redemptive sleep.

Meanwhile, the regimental doctor made a brief flying visit through the sick bay.

"I think we can fix this leg here," the regimental doctor said to the young assistant doctor as he stood in front of Aiden's bed. "But if he continues not to talk and react, then we'll have to send him on to the war hospital in Kortrijk. In this condition he is no longer fit for the front."

The young assistant doctor nodded in agreement.

"Let's wait until tomorrow to see if anything changes. Otherwise we'll send him on."

With these words, he turned around to face his next patient with the amputated arm.

Aiden didn't notice any of this. He was still asleep and only woke up hours later when a man shook him by the sleeve.

He had a tin bowl of soup and a piece of bread with him and placed it on the low wooden box that stood next to Aiden's hospital bed.

"Here is your dinner. Can you eat alone?" the man looked at him questioningly.

Aiden heard his words but understood none of them. He looked at the soup and the bread and back at the man and thought he understood what he was trying to say and nodded at the man, who then turned and left.

He looked into the tin bowl and the steaming broth rose to his nose, whereupon his stomach immediately went into turmoil and made growling noises.

Aiden straightened his upper body and carefully turned onto his side. He propped himself up on his elbow, took the tin bowl with his other hand and held it to his nose, smelling it.

"Potato soup," he called out in surprise, and was immediately startled to realise that he had spoken aloud.

Anxiously, he looked around to see if anyone had heard him. The soldier next to him, with the amputated arm, looked at him in irritation.

"Did you say something?" he asked immediately.

Aiden quickly lifted the tin bowl to his mouth, slurped some soup and ignored the man next to him.

He turned his head away again and also took his tin bowl in his right hand, which was still there, and devoted himself to his meal. But every now and then he cast a suspicious glance at Aiden.

He was sure he had heard something, but it sounded strangely alien. When he had finished his meal, he turned to Aiden.

"My name is Eugen. What is your name?"

Aiden looked up from his tin bowl. Was he talking to me, he thought, startled. He quickly lowered his head and spooned up his soup.

"Well then, don't," Eugen muttered and lay back on his hospital couch.

Aiden also put his soup bowl back on the wooden box and laid his head on the pillow.

He thought of Franz. What madness it was to go along with this proposal. How was that going to work out? They would soon become suspicious if he didn't speak. And it was only a matter of time before someone would stumble upon the truth of who he really was.

*

From now on, Aiden spent his waking hours in unspeakable fear of discovery. And he realised that this fear would now accompany him, every second.

If he managed to remain undetected here in the military hospital, he did not know what would await him in Germany. What would Franz's wife say if he suddenly appeared? Would she take him in? Or would she betray him and hand him over to the Germans?

All at once he realised that he didn't know which turn his what fate would take and the better choice would be.

Staying here would mean dying on the battlefield in all probability. Being sent to Germany because he was no longer fit for service would mean that he would survive. Albeit as a prisoner of war, if his game of lies was discovered. But someday, when the war was over, perhaps he could return to his homeland in Ireland.

At this small spark of hope, Aiden's heart began to beat loudly and he clung to this small piece of hope that he suddenly felt.

He wanted to try and remember Franz's words that he should just stay silent, not react and not say anything, then everything will take its course.

With these thoughts, he finally fell asleep again, until he suddenly felt someone put something down on his stomach. Startled, he jumped up.

The two doctors were standing in front of him and had placed two boards on his stomach.

"Here is the diagnostic board for the wounded man from Letten. First of all, we'll send him to the medical bunker at St. Quentin. There we'll see what happens to his leg.

It doesn't look too bad."

With these words, the regimental doctor addressed Aiden, who, however, again only looked at him with a puzzled expression.

"Do you hear, my boy? Your leg is not in such bad shape. We'll fix it."

Motionless, Aiden perceived the misunderstood words.

"One would think the boy doesn't understand us?" the second doctor speculated.

"Yes, it would seem so," thoughtfully and suspiciously.

the regimental surgeon looked at Aiden and raised his right hand.

Index finger to his mouth.

Aiden held his breath as he noticed the suspicious look on the regimental doctor's face. Now it will be over in a moment, now they would expose him as an enemy. Everything trembled and shook inside him until this trembling also spread to his hands, which he then quickly intertwined to keep them still.

But the regimental doctor noticed the trembling of his hands and pointed with his index finger.

"That's where they see the tremor? This indicates trauma, he explained to the still young doctor.

"Maybe he lost his speech or his hearing because of a shell? Often the shock wave also causes this trembling in the soldiers. This could explain why he is not responding," he explained to the assistant doctor. "The doctors at the military hospital in St. Quentin should clarify that. It's possible he's just faking it, like so many before him," he continued his explanations sceptically. "In any case, he is fit for transport and can be taken to the medical bunker in St. Quentin tomorrow morning," he decided. If the trembling and speechlessness don't stop, he can still be used in a replacement battalion back home if necessary. That's for his colleagues to decide."

He took the diagnostic panels from Aiden's abdomen and tore off one of each of the red perforated edges, which meant that this soldier was fit for transport, and put them back.

"And don't forget the sack with his belongings. Tie it to his healthy leg so it doesn't get lost," he ordered the young assistant doctor, who had only been on duty here at the front for a few days.

This was his first patient transport, which he was to accompany to the next larger military hospital.

The doctors turned to the nearest hospital couch and Aiden still held his hands, which were shaking like aspen leaves.

He did not know what the doctor had said, but he realised that he was not exposed and was relieved for the time being. The following night he could hardly sleep, his thoughts about his future preoccupied him so much. And every thunder of the cannons on the battlefield that he heard in the distance did the rest.

Last night it had been quieter, but today the noise of battle lasted all night.

Aiden had a faint suspicion that they were up to something with him. But what did he not know and he waited tensely to see what would happen.

*

During the night, the pain in Aiden's leg returned, and over the next few hours it stretched all the way up his body.

He lay there whimpering until finally, in the early hours of the morning, the young assistant doctor came and gave him another injection in the arm.

"This is for your pain, so you can endure the ambulance transport," the young doctor explained to him.

This time Aiden didn't fight back, knowing now that this thing the doctor was stabbing his arm with would take away his pain.

"You'll be picked up in two hours," the assistant doctor told him, looking at him questioningly, waiting for a reaction.

But Aiden just stared at him uncomprehendingly and began to tremble again. Shrugging, the doctor turned and walked away.

Then it was time. Men came to his bedside with a wooden platform, which they placed next to his bed and then lifted him onto it, not exactly gently.

Aiden cried out in pain because one of the men also grabbed him by his injured foot as they lifted him off the stretcher. Beads of sweat covered his pain-filled face.

They laid a grey, coarse woollen blanket over his body. A man tied the grey sack with Aiden's few belongings to his healthy leg and placed the diagnosis board under the blanket. Then they lifted him up and carried him out of the medical tent.

It was still early in the morning, and the air outside was permeated with wisps of mist from the onset of autumn. Cannon fire was still thundering not too far away.

Aiden was carried to an old horse-drawn cart and laid there alongside ten other injured people.

His stretcher was tied to the platform of the carriage by ropes so that it could not slip off the carriage during the bumpy ride over rough terrain.

Aiden turned his head to the side and spotted his neighbour with the amputated arm.

Eugen looked at him. Fear was in his eyes.

"Do you think they will let us go home? I want so much to go home to my wife and children. But what will they say if I come home with only one arm?" he murmured in despair and looked at Aiden, who just stared at him uncomprehendingly.

"Oh yes, you don't hear," resignedly he turned away again.

The young assistant doctor climbed up to the front of the coachman and then the journey began.

Aiden felt every bump when the wooden flatbed truck hit a deep pothole.

All the injured groaned loudly each time. It was a horror ride and how long it would last, they did not know.

Aiden's thoughts wandered back to the time when he still lived carelessly at home with his parents. He had quarreled with his sister Eimear, whom he loved more than anything and who had always looked out for him.

Suddenly he remembered the golden coin. A deep horror seized him that it might be lost. Where had he put it?

He suddenly couldn't remember. In his shoe? Or into his jacket? He quickly grabbed the sack that was tied to his leg and pulled it up to him.

He untied the ribbon and reached into the bag. There he could feel the uniform jacket. Panic overcame him. He untied the drawstring of the sack and pulled the uniform jacket halfway out and searched all the pockets.

Then he found the letter from Franz to his wife Elisabeth and was relieved that it was still there.

He kept searching, his desperation growing by the second. But finally, in one of the small inner pockets of the uniform jacket, he found the golden coin. Apparently they had not found it or had considered it worthless. Otherwise it probably wouldn't still be here.

Aiden held it in his hands, closed his eyes and thought about what the goblin had said to him about the coin.

He could still remember every single word.

You know, little boy, always keep this coin safe and always carry it with you. And if one day you are in need or in a difficult situation, take this coin in your hand and it will help you, carry you and guide you, whatever may happen.

As Aiden thought of these words, he pressed the golden coin, with his hand, even tighter against his chest.

He wanted so much to believe that everything would be all right and that he would find his way back home to his parents and his homeland.

He quickly stowed the coin safely inside the jacket. He hoped fervently that he would not lose it. It was the only thing, the only hope he had left.

*

West Front/France 1916
Saint Quentin - Field hospital
10 September

After hours of driving, with only a few breaks, the flatbed truck finally stopped. Aiden straightened up and tried to see something over the edge of the cargo bed. But he felt so exhausted that he couldn't feel his body at all and quickly dropped back.

The carriage stood in front of a large, imposing building on whose grey wall this large red cross could be seen again. It was a kind of bunker.

Many people were busily walking around in front of the building. Several trucks and more horse-drawn carriages were queuing up.

Stretchers with injured people were lifted off each vehicle and carried into the building through a wide wooden door.

A resolute woman in a nurse's uniform with a white and grey apron and a bandage with a red cross printed on the sleeve gave strict instructions to the men.

Now it was the turn of the carriage on which Aiden was lying to be unloaded.

A man joined them on the cot and untied the ropes that had held their stretchers.

Then he pushed one stretcher after the other to the front, where two men were already waiting and pulled them off the Ark.

Everything happened very quickly and ruthlessly. There was little consideration for the injured.

When it was Aiden's turn, he anxiously held onto the edges of his gurney for fear of falling off.

When it was finally done, the men, under the direction of the energetic nurse, carried him into the building.

The medical bunker in St. Quentin, where Aiden was taken, had served as a stage war hospital for two months. Here, all urgently needed operations were carried out again and the injured were sorted out.

Some who had to be sent home, those who were not fit for transport and finally those who could be nursed back to health here and then sent back to the front.

Unlike the field hospital Aiden had been in before, there were many doctors here, almost more women who were trained nurses.

Aiden was taken to a room where the new arrivals were first examined and then distributed to other large rooms depending on their diagnosis.

He felt more than helpless. He was constantly spoken to and did not understand a word, just stared impassively at the nurses.

After a while, the older, resolute nurse, who had already caught his eye when he arrived, came to his bedside and spoke to him.

She looked at him waitingly after asking for his name.

When he gave no answer, she asked again, now a little more impatient.

Aiden's gaze grew anxious under her scrutinising scrutiny and he quickly averted his eyes from her.

The nurse grabbed his arm. He looked at her again and fear was written all over his face.

"Do you understand me boy?" She bent down to him.

"My God, you really are still a young lad. How old are you?"

Again she got no answer. She looked at him suspiciously.

"Can't you understand me or don't you want to understand me?"

At that moment, a doctor came by and the nurse immediately beckoned him to Aiden's bedside.

"Well Sister Irene, what's the problem here?"

"He doesn't speak. According to the diagnosis board, his name is Franz and he has an injured leg, but it looks like it will be okay. But he doesn't answer and seems traumatised."

The doctor looked at him scrutinisingly.

"Maybe his ears are damaged and he doesn't hear anything they say to him? Write it on the board by the bed, I will look at him later. First I have to take care of the more seriously wounded. Re-bandage his leg so it doesn't get infected. And if he's in pain, give him an injection. And look on his board to see if he has been vaccinated against tetanus yet?"

The nurse nodded to the doctor and turned back to Aiden.

"Did you hear me, if you are in pain, you let me know."

But again she got no answer. Shrugging her shoulders, she turned around and set to work,

to look at the next injured person.

*

The day passed slowly for Aiden. He lay on his hospital bed, surrounded by the bustle of the nurses.

Time and again, an injured person was taken out of the room and only brought back after hours.

Some of the wounded were sitting on their beds talking to the person next to them, some were just lying there staring at the high ceiling of the grey stone room.

Others lay there with their eyes closed, whimpering in their pain.

Aiden was hungry and hoped that the sisters would bring him something to eat soon. He couldn't even ask that.

It was so frustrating for him, in this foreign environment and with these people with the foreign language he didn't understand. And the perpetual fear that he would be exposed.

Only one thought soothed him. It would still be better to be exposed and end up as a prisoner of war than to be sent back to the front to fight.

Again and again he blamed himself why he had let himself be carried away by the British soldiers to go to war.

What a gravely wrong decision he had made back then.

Quickly he tried to wipe away the cloudy thoughts, as he was aware that all the ruminating was pointless.

It happened that way and now he had to live with the consequences and try to find a way out of this chaos.

With his hand, he fished out the grey sack from under his bed.

He reached in and took out the uniform jacket and looked for the golden coin.

He looked at her for a long time, the only thing, apart from his memories, that remained from his homeland.

The only thing he could hold on to and that gave him a spark of hope.

And the longer he looked at the coin, the more he felt an energy and power within him and the awareness that he had to let himself be led and continue to persistently stand mute and deaf.

He could do nothing else, he had no other choice but to silently accept everything that is and comes and never give up hope that he would find his way back home.

How long the way back took, he did not know, but he suddenly felt within himself a certainty and a will that it would be so.

It became a little lighter in him, the tension gave way. For another moment he held the golden coin in his hands, saw his mother and father in front of him, waving at him and his sister Eimear running towards him when he came home again.

And a smile settled on his lips and lit up his whole face at his thoughts of home.

He lingered in this energy for a moment and knew, he could always get that moment back, no matter where he was.

Then he put the coin back into his uniform jacket and put the bag under his bed, closed his eyes, dreamed of his homeland in moving images and finally fell asleep.

*

The days passed.

Until now, only the nurses had taken care of his leg. The doctors were totally overloaded with operations and amputations. There seemed to be no end to the number of newly arrived wounded.

Aiden lay in his bed, asleep, dreaming, watching what was happening around him. He still could not get up.

The worst time for him was when he had to go to the toilet. He was given a bowl or a bottle with a long neck to urinate into. Aiden was so embarrassed to have to have his bottom cleaned by the nurses.

But the other soldiers were no different, and as time went by, Aiden could accept more and more that this was the case. But he hoped that he would soon be able to get up and go to the toilet himself.

Sometimes he got an injection when he was particularly restless and the pain became more severe again.

The older sister often came to his bedside and spoke to him. "I am Sister Irene. My name is Sister Irene."

Aiden understood that Irene was her name.

On impulse, he would have liked to say that his name was Aiden, but he suppressed it just in time. Franz was his name now. He had to get used to it. But he decided to continue pretending that he didn't understand anything.

The sister seemed to have him under special observation, he noticed. She often looked at him attentively and thoughtfully. Aiden became very uncertain under her gaze and always turned his face away quickly.

And although she seemed very hard and energetic at times, he trusted her and felt the desire to tell her everything. But he could not risk that.

And the language barrier would also make this impossible.

Over time, they understood each other without speaking. Sometimes she stroked his cheek with her rough, calloused hand and said something.

By the warm tone in her voice, which resembled his mother's voice when she had often comforted him, Aiden could guess that she meant well with him.

After a few days, Aiden had long since stopped counting the days, it was time to sit up in bed.

The nurses helped him, washed him thoroughly and put a new, fresh shirt on him.

They brought him two long wooden crutches and his first attempt to pull himself up seemed almost hopeless. He had no strength in his arms and sweat beaded on his forehead under the immense effort.

The sisters came to his side and grasped him under his armpits and helped him pull himself up on the crutches. When he finally stood, he laughed across his sweat-covered face.

"Well done my boy." one of the nurses said, patting him on the shoulder.

He sat back on the bed and the nurses left him alone again. But after only a few moments, ambition gripped him again and he wanted to try again and this time alone.

After a few attempts, he actually managed to pull himself up on his crutches and then stood upright, laughing all over his face.

He repeated this a few more times and was cheered on by his bedmates as he painstakingly pulled himself up by the crutches again and again. Until finally, completely exhausted, he fell back on his bed and soon fell asleep.

*

Some time later, a doctor stood by his bed and shook his arm to wake him up. He opened his eyes.

"Can you understand me?" the doctor asked.

When Aiden stared at him, the doctor shook his head.

"I think he has severe trauma from the shells. We could only determine whether his eardrum is completely destroyed by an operation. But this operation would be too costly here," he said to the nurses.

"But why doesn't he speak then?" replied Sister Irene, who was also standing by the bed.

"Yes, I'd like to know that too," he said thoughtfully, touching his chin.

"Maybe the shock triggered these symptoms without any organic damage. That happens quite often. Sometimes it can take weeks for speech and hearing to return. On the other hand, if it is a damaged eardrum and we don't react quickly, then it remains a damage that can never be repaired. I think maybe too long a time has passed for that."

The doctor considered his next course of action and pulled a metal ear trumpet from his coat pocket, holding it to Aiden's right ear.

Then he put his mouth on the opening and blew lightly into it.

Aiden immediately flinched, as his ears were perfectly fine and he didn't know what the doctor was up to with that strange thing in his hand.

"He's still responding very well. I'll try again," and he put his mouth on the opening of the ear trumpet again, but this time he spoke into the tube.

Aiden was ready for it this time and instinctively tried not to react.

But the doctor's voice could be heard through the pipe so strongly that he flinched again. The doctor repeated the same thing a few more times and found that the boy responded well.

"Well, the ears are definitely still intact. So it can't be because of his hearing that he doesn't speak."

The doctor did the same procedure on the left ear, with the same result.

Sister Irene, meanwhile, was watching Aiden closely, who also noticed.

They both looked into each other's eyes and after endless seconds for Aiden, Sister Irene suddenly winked at him conspiratorially.

"Maybe it's better if we send him back to Germany and he can heal up there in familiar surroundings," Sister Irene said, addressing the doctor who was just noting down his findings on the diagnosis board.

The latter looked up, at the sister, then at Aiden.

"Yes, that would probably make the most sense. So traumatised, he's not fit for duty at the front anyway, and here he's just blocking a bed that we urgently need for other injured people," the doctor replied.

"What about his leg?" he turned to Sister Irene again.

"It is healing very well. He's already standing up on his own with the crutches and can go to the toilet by himself," replied Nurse Irene.

"When is the next railway sick transport back to Germany?" he asked Sister Irene.

"The next one is scheduled in three days, if all goes well and the front line does not shift further to our side."

"Well then get all the papers ready and I'll sign them so he's ready to go."

"Yes, everything will be taken care of",

She took the diagnostic chart he handed her.

"His mother will be pleased," she added, smiling encouragingly at Aiden.

He watched the conversation between the doctor and the nurse the whole time and wished he could understand something. What would happen to him now? What would happen next?

*

The next day, Aiden continued to practice with his crutches and was now able to walk up and down the centre aisle between the beds a few times.

Every now and then one of the soldiers who were watching him would speak to him, but Aiden just shrugged apologetically with his shoulder.

The next morning, for the first time, he dared to leave the hospital room and go outside.

There were more ambulances in front of the building with many injured people being unloaded. There was no end to it.

Aiden lived in his own world, in his own thoughts, which continued to be full of energy and hope and were only eclipsed by his fear in a few moments.

That evening, Sister Irene came to his bedside once more and put a new bandage on him.

She also brought him new clothes. A pair of trousers and a jacket made of camouflage grey, rough fabric.

"You can go home in the morning, my boy," she chatted to him, as she put the bandage on him.

"Do you understand me, you may go home. Tomorrow morning is the day," she smiled and looked into his eyes, which stared at her uncomprehendingly.

Very close, she now bent over his face.

"you.... go... home." she whispered in his ear.

Aiden jerked his head around and stared at her, aghast and afraid. Had he just heard right? She was speaking to him in his language.

Sister Irene looked at him encouragingly.

"I guessed right. I have now tried it in English. I don't know which country you come from. But don't worry, I won't betray you," she added in German, knowing that he wouldn't understand her again.

"All.... well." she whispered in his ear again and put her right index finger to her lips to show him that his secret was safe with her.

Then she got up and left.

Aiden was confused. How had she found out?

How did she find out that he didn't speak German? That he was an enemy and that he wanted to go to Germany? She had seen through him, but he had understood that she would not betray him.

Little did he know that behind her strictness, Sister Irene had incredible intuition and perception, and she quickly saw that something was wrong with Aiden.

Especially after the doctor had diagnosed that his ears could not be too badly damaged. And she put one and one together and made up her own mind. Although of course she didn't know how it had come about that he had been brought in as a German soldier.

She wondered if the boy had come up with the idea himself. was to pose as an injured German or whether someone, a German soldier, had helped him to do so.

She knew only one thing, this boy had taken his chance. And she couldn't blame him for wanting to escape this cruelty.

However that was going to happen. And she wanted to help him do that. She wanted to give him a chance.

Sadly, she thought of her fallen husband and her son, who was still fighting out there somewhere.

*

Not even a year had passed when she received the news that her husband had been killed here on the Western Front. They lived in Berlin. Sister Irene was a head nurse at the Charité in Berlin.

After this death notice, nothing kept her there any more, because her son was also on duty here on the Western Front. And she wanted to be near him and work here in the war hospital.

Every day she prayed for her son and also for the many thousands of soldiers and yet she knew that she could not prevent too many men from dying in the battles and perhaps her son too.

Sister Irene was a very strong woman, but inside she had a very soft core, which she rarely showed.

But here with this boy, who reminded her so much of her own son when he was this age, this side came out and she wanted to help him, no matter who he was or what country he came from.

For Sister Irene there were no enemies. For her, there were only people who were all equal and deserved the same help. She thought of his mother, who must have been in agony if she did not hear from her son, as she often experienced for weeks when she received no sign of life from her husband before he had fallen and was now eagerly awaiting any news of her son. She would like to help this boy even more and would have liked to send a letter for him to his country, to his mother.

But it was simply too dangerous. The letters abroad were all checked. And so she shared his secret and wished that whatever detours he had to take, he would find his way home again.

*

The next morning was the day. Aiden was to be woken up before sunrise, but he had already been lying awake in his bed for a long time.

Sister Irene came to his bedside with two men and took the diagnosis board.

"Here, you have to take these as well. These are the papers and we tied the bag with his things to his healthy leg. Be careful. His name is Franz, but he doesn't speak. He is severely traumatised, as you can read on the diagnosis board," she called imperiously to the two men.

Then she stepped next to Aiden, stroking his cheek again. With her eyes she tried to encourage him.

"I wish you all the best, my boy. You're going to Heidelberg first and from there to Munich," she told him. "I know you don't understand me," she replied to his perplexed look.

Then she wanted to leave, but Aiden held her back by her hand

and squeezed them tightly and pulled them towards her. Sister Irene bent low over his face.

"Thank you for everything," he whispered in her ear and gave her a kiss on the cheek.

Sister Irene looked at him and wiped a few tears from the corners of her eyes.

She rose quickly and hurried away. It was not good to allow too many feelings in these times.

Then everything happened very quickly. Aiden was again tied to the bed of an ambulance with a stretcher. There were many other injured people there and they were taken to a railway station not far away and loaded onto a train that would take them to Germany. The sun was just rising when the train started moving.

*

Heidelberg, Germany
War hospital
30 September 1916

Excitement gripped Aiden among all the German soldiers. He found no distraction as he could not talk to his fellow soldiers. He was often spoken to, to which he just shrugged his shoulders and pointed to his ears.

Now that he was on the train on his way to Germany, his thoughts often revolved around the question of how Elisabeth, Franz's wife, would react.

He had overcome the first hurdles. Now he was getting closer and closer to meeting Franz's wife.

Would she betray him? Would she be able to trust him when he told her how he had met Franz and how he had suggested this role reversal to him before he died?

However, Aiden knew he had no choice. She was the only point of contact he had there in Germany. And Franz, in his last minutes, firmly trusted that his wife would help him.

The journey had now lasted several hours. The train stopped several times, sometimes longer, sometimes only for a few minutes. Aiden was lying in a goods wagon with many men, crammed into a very small space. Only through a few air vents did some fresh air enter the wagon.

The floor was thickly covered with straw, on which lay coarse, grey woollen blankets.

The passenger wagons were only available for the higher-ranking officers, and since there were no longer any rank insignia on his uniform jacket, as Franz had torn it off, he found himself in the goods wagon with the common soldier folk.

He thought of the short time he had spent with Franz in that bomb crater.

But even if it was only this short time, he knew that he had met a big-hearted person there. A miracle, he kept thinking. He would probably already be dead if he hadn't met Franz in this threatening situation.

Sometimes Aiden would fall asleep for a short time, only to be woken up again by squeaking railway wheels.

His leg was getting better and better. He still had a little pain, but it was easy to bear.

He felt that it would be all right again.

He realised that the fact that he was supposedly unable to speak and hear gave him the luck, the miracle, of being sent home, as he was so unfit for action at the front.

But sometimes it wasn't easy, because in his own world and his loneliness, he almost went crazy.

How he would love to talk to someone, to tell someone about his homeland and his family.

But he knew it was not possible until he had reached Franz's wife and then it was also uncertain whether she wanted to understand him.

Franz had told her that she also knew his language, but would she want to listen to him?

Over and over again, his thoughts circled incessantly, turning as if in a hamster wheel that does not come to a standstill.

After a few hours of travel, the train stopped and the carriage doors were opened. Aiden took a deep breath of the oxygen that flowed in through the large opening. He lifted his head and saw that thick grey clouds covered the sky.

They were at a railway station, he guessed, as there were still some stationary trains on the other tracks.

When he had been shipped from Ireland to England by ship, they were taken to a large railway station immediately afterwards, he remembered, as he now saw the many tracks and wagons standing there.

To this day he does not know the name of the place. They were shipped like animals and immediately herded into a big, long train, crammed into the wagons and taken to the ship at the other end of England, where they were then ferried to France.

It had all been new to him. He had only seen a train once before, when he was in Dublin with his parents. But it was nothing like the size and length of these trains.

The cargo ship on which he crossed the Irish Sea months ago had fascinated him very much and there he still felt like an adventurer going on a great journey.

Where this journey was leading to, he had no idea at the time. If he could have even guessed, he would certainly have been less euphoric.

Now they were standing in a station with the hatch open. The other injured soldiers were all talking in confusion and those who could get up went to the large opening and watched what was going on out there. Aiden was still lying down, even though he desperately needed to go to the bathroom. He waited until the first people got out of the wagon, then he straightened up and crawled with his arms over the straw towards the open door. He dragged his crutches behind him.

When he got there, he sat up and carefully swung his feet over the edge. By now he had enough strength in his arms again to support himself on the crutches. He placed them on the ground and carefully let himself slide off the edge of the train, his arms firmly resting on the crutches.

Then he looked around. Where could he do his business? He saw some men standing opposite on another train who were also urgently relieving themselves.

He copied them and then returned to his wagon and continued to look around.

First, the injured who had got off the train were treated, then the injured who were on the train were treated.

His stomach growled pitifully and he was immensely thirsty. After a while, a group of men came. Two of them carried a huge vat from which thick steam rose.

The others carried boxes with tin cups and mugs, still others carried large canisters that probably contained water, he hoped.

Relief rose in him. Finally something to drink, he thought.

From the big vat, the men distributed a thin potato soup and everyone got a big piece of bread to go with it, as well as a cup full of water from the canisters.

Some needed help because they couldn't even hold the tin bowl without spilling everything. Others could not sit up and had to be fed by the spoonful.

Aiden sat down on the floor in front of the train and frantically fell over the soup, greedily chewing the bread with it after finishing the cup of water in one go.

Thank God he was given another cup of water. He would have liked to have had some of the soup more, but the ration was just enough for all the soldiers in the wagon to which he belonged.

But for now, the worst hunger and thirst had been quenched and after the men had collected all the tin cups and mugs again, they were herded back into the wagon.

Aiden felt like the sheep at home, which he often had to drive out to pasture.

When he had reached his place again, he put the crutches on the straw and carefully settled down.

Some more time passed before the large carriage door was finally closed. Aiden heard the whistle and the steam emitting from the steam engine and the train slowly started to move.

Soon he fell asleep, under the monotonous rattling of the iron wheels on the rails.

*

The dream

Birdsong accompanied him as he soared over the rolling, lush green hills of the Hills of Tara. He spread his arms wide and floated around like a big bird until he reached the tree under which an old, grey wooden bench stood.

He saw that his mother was sitting there on the bench, crying bitterly into her stained apron. Tears also came to his eyes and he immediately wanted to sit with her and comfort her. But he could not reach the ground. Again and again he was carried away by the wind, which blew stormily up there most of the time.

And while he had just found this floating over the green hills of his homeland very beautiful, panic suddenly rose in him. He wanted to go to his mother and couldn't. He tried to shout something out loud so that she could see him, but his voice failed and his words were carried away by the wind.

Again and again he tried, but he did not succeed.

Suddenly his mother lifted her head and looked into the old, dry branches of the tree, stood up, pulled out of her apron pocket a small piece of cloth attached to a thin string and tied it to a branch of the tree. Immediately the wind blew through the branches and the piece of cloth fluttered in the wind. She reached out once more with her hand and stroked it. Then she made her way down the hill to the cottage where work awaited her. Aiden knew this was a rag tree, as they called such trees in Ireland.

These were so-called wish trees. You attach a piece of cloth or paper with a request or a wish to the branches of the tree and hoped that the wind would take the wish to heaven.

Aiden watched everything from the air high above and did his rounds above the tree.

What had his mother tied to the tree there, he asked himself? He hovered very close to this branch to which the piece of cloth was tied. There were only a few words written on it in the old Gaelic language *'Dia duit mo mhac. Tar abhaile go sláintiúil. (God bless you my son. Come home safe and sound.)'*

Aiden knew that his mother, like him, liked to be up on the Hills of Tara, where that wishing tree was.

Since time immemorial, Tara was considered the seat of the legendary high kings and carried many stories and legends on its hills. He thought of the many evenings when he listened to his mother's tales.

Sadness and deep longing for his family gripped his heart. But at that moment, the tree, all the scraggy branches, burst into flames and thick smoke took his breath away. He tried to fly away, but he could not. He whirled around in the flames above the tree and the smoke entered his lungs and threatened to suffocate him.

*

Aiden opened his eyes. Acrid smoke took his breath away. He gasped for air, over and over again. Where was he? Just a moment ago he had been over the Hills of Tara. That was where he had seen his mother.

He wanted to get up, but could not. Each time he fell back with a coughing fit and gasped for air. The shouting of the men around him grew louder and louder, but no gunfire could be heard. Where was he?

Suddenly he was pulled up by the shoulders and saw thick, brown smoke in front of his eyes and he could hardly see his surroundings because of the coughing.

The men's shouting became more and more frantic and louder until suddenly, with a powerful jolt, the train stopped and all the men who had already stood up fell to the ground. The men scrambled up, coughing, and pulled at the carriage door to open it.

Aiden was so confused that he still didn't realise he was no longer dreaming He couldn't see anything in this thick smoke.

Then finally the carriage door opened and the men who were already in front of the door quickly jumped out, fell to the ground and gasped for breath.

Aiden acted instinctively, still gasping for breath, and crawled towards the exit.

Suddenly he really woke up and realised that he was on the train to Germany and not in the skies above the Hills of Tara. What had happened?

Had the train been fired at.

Aiden had often heard of trains and ships being fired upon to prevent the enemy from resupplying soldiers.

Aiden was lying on his stomach towards the open carriage door, where he was grabbed under the shoulders by a man who had rushed up and dragged him out of the carriage.

He cried out loudly. His injured leg scraped over the edge of the carriage and a hellish pain ran through him, starting from his leg and running through his entire body. At the same time, he continued to gasp for air until he finally lay exhausted on the floor in front of the train, gasping for breath.

He only noticed the hustle and bustle around him again after a few minutes.

He sat up and when he looked at the open wagon door he saw that the straw in the wagon was smoking and partly glowing.

A fire had broken out. But how could that happen, Aiden asked himself.

He saw them pull two men out of the wagon. They were lying motionless on the stretchers. They were set down outside and a man in a white coat hurried over. He knelt down, felt the men's pulse at the carotid artery, but shook his head.

Blankets were brought and the two men were covered with them.

Aiden watched in shock. What had happened? Why had the fire broken out?

Uniformed soldiers approached and in a stern tone they questioned the men standing around. They pointed angrily with their fingers at a man who was still sitting on the ground and coughing.

The uniformed soldiers approached the man and pulled him up by his arms. They shouted at him, but he continued to cough and kept his head down.

Aiden wondered again what had happened? Then he saw the uniformed men searching through the man's clothes and finally found what they were looking for and pulled out a crumpled packet of cigarettes and matches.

Now Aiden realised a few things. The man had smoked on the train and used it to ignite the dry straw, which is how the fire started.

Meanwhile, some men were pushing the smouldering straw out of the wagon. Aiden, as well as some others, moved further to the side so as not to be exposed to this smoking smoke again.

The man they had found the pack of cigarettes on, despite his injuries to his arms and legs, was ruthlessly pulled up and taken away. Aiden looked after them and watched as they hoisted him into another wagon and tied him down.

Meanwhile, the smoky wagon was being emptied. Men came with a wooden cart full of straw and blankets. The straw was quickly distributed in the wagon and the blankets laid out.

It was still grey in the wagon from all the smoke. But there was no alternative.

The train was full to capacity and they had to return to the stinking carriage willy-nilly. But to get more fresh air, they left the carriage door open a crack and fresh air came in during the journey.

Aiden lay on his blanket and fell asleep again, exhausted. He didn't know how much longer the journey was going to take and a part of him almost wished it would take forever more because his fear of arriving in Germany and what awaited him there was growing.

Hours later, the train stopped again. Water was distributed in each wagon, but no one was allowed to leave.

What Aiden didn't know was that they had now reached the border with Germany.

The train started moving again.

And the final stretch of the journey into the unknown began for Aiden.

*

Arrival Heidelberg, Germany

02 October 1916

After a few hours, during which Aiden mostly dozed off, the train stopped again. But it was some time before the carriage door was fully opened and a soldier called something into the carriage.

Aiden watched the other injured people, who all looked at each other with relief and then burst into cheers. Some hugged each other or burst into tears laughing. They had come home.

Aiden held back and waited to see what would happen to him now.

After some time, four men suddenly stood in front of the open wagon. They shouted instructions inside the wagon in a barking voice.

One by one, they were then taken out of the wagon and joined the stream of people moving towards the small station building.

Aiden straightened up, picked up his crutches and backpack, with his belongings, and crawled to the carriage door when it was his turn.

Two of the men grabbed him under the arms and pulled him roughly out of the wagon.

Standing outside, he hung his backpack on his shoulder before leaning on his crutches and following the flow of people.

In front of a building made of red bricks stood various carts, on which a large red cross was again printed on the carriage doors, as he had now seen many times before.

Aiden waited his turn. He looked around and spotted a large white sign. He tried to decipher the letters on it.

Slowly he lined up one letter next to the other and then formed the word into a whole with his lips.

'Heidelberg' he finally whispered. Was that the name of the city he was in at the moment?

*

Aiden learned to read and write from his mother Eileen when he was a child. She loved books more than anything and had grown up in Dublin in a family of teachers where she had learned to read and write.

Aiden's father, who later became her husband, Farell Mc Gilles, had met her on a family trip to the Hill of Tara.

She had just been 18 and had gone to a pub there with her parents and Farell was just meeting his friends there for a Guinness.

Both were still very young, but a few glances they exchanged were enough for them to fall in love with each other immediately.

Farell approached the pretty girl, in the presence of her parents, and boldly asked for a date.

And a week later, Farell drove his parents' horse and cart to Dublin, visited his beloved and took her out.

From that day on they were inseparable and only six months later Farell asked for Eileen's hand in marriage and made her his wife, taking her to the cottage with him,

that lay beneath the Hills of Tara.

Aiden's mother's parents were not very pleased that their

daughter wanted to marry a simple country boy, but eventually the young people had their way. Even the prospect of a poor life in a simple cottage in solitude could not deter Eileen from marrying.

She had found the second half of her soul in Farell, as she often told Aiden and his sister Eimear with a smile.

And she would have given up everything for him, not only her city life, which she had never regretted.

They were poor, but happy together and no one could take this wealth away from them.

Aiden learned the letters quickly and often wished he had had more opportunity and books to read.

But there were few books at home and the ones that were available he did not understand at that time as a child.

He read them anyway, just to improve his reading more and more.

When he turned twelve, his parents gave him a book of old sagas and legends about Ireland for his birthday.

The book was about leprechauns and fairies, which excited him very much. He often climbed the Hills of Tara looking for the leprechaun from whom the coins had rolled to his feet at that time. Aiden often had to think of him.

But they never met again and sometimes, when he thought about it, he believed that he had only imagined it and that his imagination had played a trick on him.

But the golden coin he still possessed made him doubt again and again that it had all come from his imagination.

*

While he was still studying the white sign saying Heidelberg, it was time for him to be called to one of the trucks that were already standing by. Another soldier helped him and pushed him from behind onto the loading area, on which wooden planks were attached to the left and right so that they could sit next to each other.

Aiden propped himself up on his crutches so that he had enough support after he had found a place.

When the loading area was finally full, the vehicle started moving.

They were all talking excitedly. Aiden would have liked to understand what the men were talking about.

But he had to resign himself again to being completely at the mercy and without knowledge of what was happening now.

As the tarpaulin of the hold in which Aiden was sitting had not been closed at the back, he could see out from under the ride.

They were apparently in a larger city, because the streets they drove through were densely lined with houses.

The city seemed to have been largely spared the cruel effects of the war.

There were hardly any bombed houses and streets. In some places people stood and waved at them and the wounded soldiers waved happily back.

Aiden held back, feeling like a fraud. He, as an enemy against whose country he had fought, could not wave back at these people. So he bowed his head and tried to calm his thoughts. Then he saw that they were crossing a large magnificent bridge that led over a wide river.

Aiden had never seen such a magnificent bridge. He liked the city right away.

Was this the town where Franz lived with his wife? Aiden didn't know, he was often so confused that he could only remember a little of what he had read in German.

He reached into the inside pocket of his jacket, took out the letter and deciphered the address written on it again. It said Munich. So he hadn't arrived yet, because this city was called Heidelberg, as he had read on the sign earlier.

Finally they stopped in front of a large, stately building. Flanked on the left and right by magnificent wings with pointed roofs. In the middle was a long balcony built on stone pillars, under which was the two-winged entrance, reached by means of an imposing, curved staircase.

Slowly the loading area emptied. One by one, sisters received them and many needed help to climb the curved stairs.

Aiden leaned on his crutches and hoisted himself up one step at a time.

Another nurse was already waiting upstairs, who took him by the arm and led him into the building.

There was a large hall in which white iron beds were lined up. In between there were always small wooden tables where the injured sat and talked or played cards.

Aiden was taken to one of the beds and relieved, he sat down.

Exhaustion overtook him after the long train ride. His leg hurt like hell and he hoped he would soon get something for the pain. He heaved his backpack with his belongings onto the bed on top of a grey woollen blanket partially wrapped in a white sheet.

Another middle-aged nurse came to his bedside and brought him a plate of stew and a piece of bread, as well as a cup of water. Aiden gave her a friendly nod of thanks and smiled at her.

"How old are you, my boy?" she asked him in a warm voice. He shrugged his shoulder again in despair, as he had done so often in recent weeks.

Full of compassion, the sister looked at him and pointed at herself.

"My name is Jutta. Jutta! Do you understand?" she looked at him questioningly.

Aiden guessed that she wanted to tell him her name. However, he did not dare to repeat the name, but only nodded his head.

He reached into his jacket pocket and pulled out Franz's letter and showed it to the sister, which said Franz von Letten as the sender. At the same time, Aiden pointed at himself to show her that he was Franz.

The nurse nodded.

"You are Franz. Welcome here in Heidelberg. Well then, let me see your diagnosis board."

With her hand she pointed a rectangle in the air.

Aiden immediately understood what she meant and pulled up his bag, took out the diagnostic chart and handed it to the nurse.

"Ahh, yes, you don't hear and you don't speak. That's why you don't react," Sister Jutta muttered to herself while she studied the blackboard.

Aiden watched her and looked at her a little more closely. She wore a clean white apron over an ankle-length grey dress. On the sleeve of the dress was a bandage again with a red cross.

Her brown hair was tied softly into a loose mop of hair away from her face. On her head she wore a white nurse's cap.

Aiden estimated that she must be about the same age as his mother. She looked very nice, Aiden thought, and also reminded him of Sister Irene in the field hospital, although she was several years older.

So far, Aiden had only had good experiences with the Germans. First Franz, then Sister Irene and now Sister Jutta. Aiden thought that a good star was probably watching over him. Or did the golden coin have something to do with it?

And for a small moment, gratitude flooded through him. Despite all the cruelty, he felt gratitude at that moment because he had been given this opportunity to possibly survive this terrible war.

Sister Jutta put a hand on his shoulder.

"Are you all right?" she looked sympathetically into his tear-soaked eyes.

Aiden nodded and wiped the tears vigorously from the corners of his eyes.

The nurse hung the diagnostic charts on his bed and helped him out of his jacket.

Then she brought him a pair of grey long johns and a grey shirt and indicated that he should change first and then lie down.

"Are you in pain?" she asked him, pointing at his leg and contorting her face to show him what she meant.

Aiden understood and nodded again.

"I'll get you a painkiller right away. I'll be right back."

Slowly he undressed, put on the clothes in front of him and lay down on the bed and immediately fell asleep.

Only very briefly did he wake up again when he felt a pain in his arm from the pain injection that Sister Jutta gave him. Then he slept on, exhausted.

*

When Aiden woke up again, it was already evening. The oil lamps were burning everywhere and he took a closer look at the large hall.

Only now did he notice that there was a balcony all around the hall, supported by brick pillars. Stucco and ornaments adorned the walls and the high ceiling.

The floor had once been covered with what must have been noble parquet, but was now dulled and covered with a grey patina.

Aiden got up, took his crutches and went in search of the toilet.

He left the hall and looked around. New casualties were still being brought into the building and there was a hustle and bustle.

Nurses and doctors walked around or sat tiredly at tables, their heads in their hands and their eyes closed.

In passing, a nurse showed him the way to the toilets.

When he arrived back at his bedside, there was a bowl of the same stew that had been there when he arrived.

Hungrily, Aiden made a beeline for the food. He washed down the dry bread with the cup of water that stood next to the food.

So he spent two days in his bed without being examined by a doctor.

Once a day, a nurse came and gave him an injection and re-bandaged his leg. This was all done quietly and without words, as everyone already knew that he could not speak or hear anything.

Every now and then he went outside on his crutches and enjoyed the single golden rays of sunshine that now, at the beginning of October, adorned autumn.

Aiden didn't even know if he had a voice anymore, as he hadn't spoken a word out loud for so long.

But he had no choice. In his thoughts he often imagined that someone would get the idea that he did not speak because he perhaps did not know the language and had crept in as an enemy.

But so far this had not really happened, except that he sometimes felt suspicious glances directed at him.

As he walked outside in the park once again, he saw fallen leaves everywhere and the green colour of the meadows seemed to be losing its strength.

Aiden thought of his native Ireland and the evergreen, lush meadows and hills. Also of the beautiful, intense colours that nature showed there in autumn. Incredible homesickness and longing spread through his chest.

He quickly wiped the dull thoughts away, turned around and went back into the hospital room.

*

After another two weeks, which he spent mainly lonely in his makeshift bed or taking short walks in the park in front of the military hospital, he was picked up by Sister Jutta shortly after breakfast.

She pressed his crutches into Aiden's hand and indicated that he should come along. He only needed the crutches to support his injured leg, which had already healed well.

She took him to a separate room, with a makeshift couch on which he sat down.

Shortly afterwards, a man wearing a doctor's coat came into the room.

He sat down wordlessly at the desk where Aiden's diagnostic chart lay, which Sister Jutta had taken with her.

Aiden watched the doctor expectantly, but also anxiously.

"Yes, what do we have here? Sister Jutta, how does his leg look?"

"It's healing well, doctor. He still gets a shot of painkiller every day. Penicillin is no longer necessary."

"Then let's have a look at it. Please take off the bandage so I can examine the leg."

Nurse Jutta went to Aiden and pushed him back a little with her hand on his shoulder to indicate that he should lie down. She took off the bandage on the injured leg.

The doctor stepped up to the couch and examined the leg.

"Yes, that looks good. Wrap it up again, please. And it's really enough if you just give him some mild painkillers. That, I think, is enough."

He turned around and went back to his desk.

"Sister Jutta, I don't understand why he was sent here to Heidelberg? The leg will soon be fine. He can certainly go back to the front in a month or two. I'm very surprised about that now. He is still so young and in his manhood and can still serve the Fatherland," the doctor looked at Aiden in amazement.

"But Doctor Meinges, haven't you read. The patient obviously no longer speaks or hears."

Sister Jutta went to Doctor Meinges at the desk and showed him the clue on the diagnostic board.

"As far as I know, the ears have already been checked for a damaged eardrum, but this has been ruled out as he reacted to sounds and to air. He seems to have succumbed to a trauma that has left him speechless."

"Well, let's do some more tests here," Doctor Meinges decided and rose to go back to the couch where Aiden was lying.

He performed various tests on the ears, to which Aiden always responded, however hard he tried not to.

Finally, the doctor came with a huge syringe and nurse Jutta held a bowl under Aiden's head.

"I'll give his ears a good rinse, maybe some dirt has collected there and limited his hearing? Which doesn't explain his speechlessness, of course. But it won't do any harm. Maybe it will go away on its own.

The doctor explained to Aiden what he was going to do, but of course he didn't understand him. Even though he now knew some German words that he had picked up from the injured or the nurses, which he could also assign to what they meant, he could not yet follow any conversation or explanation.

But he saw what the doctor was up to. In this huge syringe was water, which he squirted into his ears, so that Aiden wanted to scream out loud because of the horrible feeling in his ears. But he suppressed it with tremendous effort.

After the examination, Aiden limped back to his bed on his crutches and lay down.

His ears still felt like a whole waterfall was rushing through and in his head he felt a slight dizziness.

At the same time, Sister Jutta was still at Doctor Meinges' desk waiting for further instructions regarding the patient Franz von Letten.

"I issue a provisional discharge note for the patient from Letten. As long as he does not speak and apparently does not hear and it has not been clarified why, he can go home. It may well be that his psyche has suffered a very strong trauma which is having this effect. However, his leg has healed well," he explained to the nurse as he eagerly filled out a document with his head down, which he handed to the nurse.

Then he turned to Sister Jutta with a questioning look.

"Do you have any suspicions about this boy?" he looked at her warily.

"What do you mean?" she looked at him in surprise.

"Well, it could also be that he's fooling us. Maybe he doesn't understand us at all? You know what I mean? «

Sister Jutta opened her eyes and shook her head in disbelief. "You think he's just pretending not to hear and not to be able to speak? Or even that he comes from an enemy camp? No, I can't believe that. He was in the field hospital for some time and if there had been indications of that, then they would surely have noticed it there and exposed him."

Doctor Meinges shrugged his shoulders.

"I just thought because there was no evidence regarding the ears that he had any damage. And he didn't seem very confused either, which would indicate psychological trauma," the doctor explained thoughtfully.

"I can't believe that, with the boy. He's still so young and what good would it do him. He would be all alone and on his own. How could he get by without knowing German? No, I definitely don't believe that," replied Sister Jutta.

"Well, it was just a thought. It often happens that soldiers desert or defect in order to turn themselves in as prisoners of war and thus escape the fighting at the front."

"No, doctor, I can't imagine that with this boy. He would certainly have been found out long ago," replied Sister Jutta with conviction.

"Yes, as you think. But please pay more attention to indications in this regard. You never know. Oh, I just saw, we have an address here in Munich. Well, then it's probably right. Please inform his family that they can receive him in Munich in the next few days."

"Yes, I will, doctor. I think we will have to put him on a train, as he cannot communicate at the station," replied Sister Jutta.

"Yes, please take care of it," Doctor Meinges replied and left the room to attend to a new patient.

Meanwhile, Nurse Jutta went to Aiden's bedside with the doctor's letter and the discharge note.

"You can go home, boy," she told him, not without studying his reactions carefully. Was there perhaps something to Doctor Meinges' suspicions after all? She could not get the thought out of her head.

"Here I have your discharge slip."

She held it up in front of Aiden's face so he could read it. Startled, he jerked back. Then he took the note in his hand and pretended to read it.

"I'm going to tell your family that you're going to Munich tomorrow on the midday train and that

they can pick you up there at the station. Elisabeth von Letten, is that your mother? You're still a bit young to be a married, aren't you?" Sister Jutta looked at Aiden questioningly. He just gave her an exasperated look, grabbed his ears and shrugged his shoulders.

"Never mind, I'll take you to the train tomorrow and send a telegram to Munich first."

She turned and was about to hurry away, but then turned back to Aiden.

"I'll come back tomorrow and help you wash and dress and re-bandage your foot again."

Aiden was irritated.

What did the sister want? He had only understood the word Munich.

He looked at the note again carefully and tried to decipher the words, which he succeeded in doing, but these words had no meaning for him because he did not understand them.

Did this mean that the time had come? That he would go to Munich to see Elisabeth von Letten?

Whenever he thinks of the upcoming encounter with Elisabeth, panic overtook him.

Aiden was aware that her reaction to him would determine his future. If she betrayed him, his deception would be exposed and then he would be at the mercy of a prisoner of war.

No one would believe him that the real Franz von Letten had suggested to him in his last hour to swap roles so that he, Aiden, could save himself.

His thoughts went round and round in circles and he found no answer. The answer, he knew, he would only get when he arrived in Munich.

*

The next morning, Nurse Jutta came to his bedside again and bandaged his leg.
She also had a bowl of warm water with her, as well as a cloth. She also had a new pair of grey uniform trousers and a shirt tucked under her arm, which she placed on the bed with him.
Then she first put a screen around his bed so that he could wash and change somewhat protected from the gaze of the other men in the hall.
Aiden was no longer embarrassed when a nurse helped him wash. He just let everything happen.
"This afternoon I'll put you on the train to Munich. I've already sent the telegram to your family," she explained to Aiden, who just looked at her uncomprehendingly.
"This afternoon... by train... home.... Munich. Do you understand me?" she tried again to tell him that he may go home.
Aiden again only understood the word Munich and simply nodded in agreement.
After Sister Jutta had removed the screen again, Aiden sat on the bed dressed. He put one and one together and understood that the fact that he had received clothes meant that he was allowed to go to Munich.
He pulled his bag with his belongings out from under the bed, which also contained his uniform jacket.

There he took out the letter and his coin.

So he sat there for a while, staring at both.

He held the coin very tightly in his left hand until the golden metal became quite warm.

He closed his eyes and murmured a prayer almost silently, thinking of his family and hoping to see them all again.

He quickly stowed everything back in the inside pocket of his uniform jacket and lay back on the bed, waiting to see what would happen now.

A few hours later, after the trays with lunch had been collected again, Sister Jutta came to his bedside.

"So my boy. Here we go."

Sister Jutta indicated that he should take his jacket and backpack and held out his crutches to him.

Aiden stood up and followed her with the bag hanging on his shoulder. He had put on his jacket.

They went outside and a flatbed truck was waiting in front of the door.

Aiden looked up at the sky and saw that the October sun was casting a golden glow on the beautiful autumn day. The air still felt cool and raw.

I wonder what the date is today? He had no idea how much time he had spent in the military hospitals and on the train since he had been picked up on the battlefield.

Surely more than a month must have passed, but perhaps more time had passed than he thought.

He only knew that this cruel day of fighting in the Battle of the Sommé took place on 6 September, his birthday. Everything that happened afterwards played out like a timeless film in which he played along, as the main protagonist. He willingly let himself drift through this film that would determine his future.

Aiden hopped with his crutches down the steps of the staircase that led from the large portal door of the building into the car park. Sister Jutta supported him as he hoisted himself onto the platform of the car with his arms and handed his crutches up to him.

She herself sat down at the front next to the driver and gave the instruction that he should please take her to the station in Heidelberg.

Once there, Sister Jutta handed Aiden an envelope with his diagnostic chart and indicated that he should put it in his backpack.

She put him on a bench and went into the station building. There she got a ticket from the attendant in charge.

The train attendant issued her a ticket and she went back to Aiden. She pressed the ticket into his hand, pulled him up by the sleeve and walked with him to the platform. Sister Jutta indicated to him that it would be another 15 minutes before the train arrived.

Silently, they stood next to each other on the platform and Aiden felt fear rising inside him. Sister Jutta noticed and gave his hand an encouraging squeeze.

"You can do it, boy. For sure."

She looked at him scrutinisingly.

"Even though I don't know what exactly is wrong with you. I do have an idea what your speechlessness is all about. But don't worry, I won't betray you." She squeezed his hand again conspiratorially and winked at him.

Aiden looked at Sister Jutta in irritation, but her warm

expression reassured him and gratefully he did not want to let go of her hand, even though he did not understand her words. But he felt that she had probably seen through him just as Sister Irene had done in the Field hospital. These women could not be fooled so easily.

And again he was lucky to have met a good soul who had not betrayed him.

Aiden could hardly believe his luck. The Germans were so different from the way his comrades at the front had berated them.

He realised that they were also very warm and good people here. Why should it be any different here than in his country or the many other countries.

Then the train pulled in. Sister Jutta climbed in front of him up two iron steps, into the train. Aiden followed her, leaning on his crutches.

Once in the compartment, she sat Aiden down on a wooden bench,

She put a small lunch packet into his hand, which she pulled out of her bag, stroked his cheek briefly and said goodbye to him.

"Come home safe, boy. Wherever that may be. God's blessings on your way."

Aiden blinked away the tears that were welling up and he reached out and looked at her gratefully.

A short time later, after Sister Jutta had left the train, the steam engine blew a strong whistle and the train slowly started moving.

When he looked out of the window, Sister Jutta waved at him and he also raised his arm and waved back.

Arrival Munich

28 October 1916

Sister Jutta had instructed the conductor to help Aiden at Stuttgart station, where he had to change to another train to Munich, and show him the way.

She also informed the conductor that the ex-soldier could not speak or hear.

Aiden had been on the train for a few hours when it stopped in front of a large station building.

He didn't move from the spot and looked out of the window straining not to be spoken to by other passengers. Inside, he was so excited that he kept holding his trembling hands. He didn't know how long the journey would take, where he would arrive or whether he would have to get off now.

Suddenly the conductor came and pulled Aiden roughly by the sleeve of his jacket behind him and hurriedly took him to the railway track next to it.

"You'll have to wait here for about an hour until the train comes to Munich. The conductor shouted in his ear, hoping that he might understand something. But Aiden only looked at him helplessly.

The conductor shrugged his shoulders and walked away. He would get on when the train came, he thought indifferently. Aiden stopped, leaning on his crutches, and waited. He decided to just get on the next train that stopped here, hoping it would be the right one.

After some time he again heard the whistle of a steam locomotive and saw a train in the distance approaching the station. By now, many people were standing around waiting for the train.

No one paid any attention to him and Aiden was happy not to be spoken to out of fear.

When the time came for the train to stop in front of the station, the waiting people crowded towards the doors, which were immediately opened from the inside.

But before they could get on, some passengers wanted to get off first, so there was a terrible crowd.

Aiden was being pushed back and forth and he was struggling to keep his balance on his crutches as he still couldn't stand properly on his injured leg. Suddenly, from behind, a small boy shot between Aiden's legs and those of the person next to him and knocked Aiden's right crutch away so that he had to step on his injured leg to avoid falling. He cried out loudly in pain and unthinkingly uttered a Gaelic swear word several times.

"Feck, Feck, Feck!"

Aiden's eyes widened in shock.

His crutch had hit the man standing in front of him with full force, who in turn had pushed the man in front of him forward. Anger arose and everyone turned indignantly to Aiden.

All the other people around him also looked at him in surprise and for a brief moment the jostling stopped and everyone stood still.

Aiden froze fearfully. The boy also stopped and looked guiltily at Aiden.

This happened within seconds. Then the boy suddenly bent down, lifted the crutch and gave it back to Aiden.

"Sorry, I didn't mean to," he shouted and disappeared in a flash between the legs of the adults in the jostling crowd.

A woman standing next to Aiden began to rant loudly.

Aiden didn't know if she meant him or the boy, but she looked after the boy.

"Are you all right?" she then asked, turning to Aiden.

He did not understand what the woman was saying, but her friendly expression told him that she meant no harm. And so he nodded, pulling his grey felt cap deeper into his face, which still showed the expression of pain that he bravely tried to breathe away. No one spoke to him again, but a few suspicious glances remained on him, even as the crowd started moving again.

Aiden's tension grew more and more.

As he sat on the train, where he had struggled to get a seat, he still felt suspicious glances on him. A couple whispered something softly to each other, keeping their eyes on him.

What if they were to confront and address him directly now? He quickly packed his backpack into the luggage net above his head, sat down and closed his eyes.

Even though he couldn't fall asleep from excitement, he kept his eyes tightly shut with effort.

The train started, whistling loudly with every burst of steam. The passengers talked in confusion, some just sat and looked out of the window, some unpacked their baskets and ate something.

Aiden thought of the package that Sister Jutta had given him and would have liked to unwrap it now, but he was afraid to open his eyes and stand up.

*

115

The train stopped a few times. People got off and others got on. His seatmates had thankfully changed and there was no one left who had witnessed this situation at the station earlier.

Now Aiden had opened his eyes.

At every stop he looked out of the window in panic, because he couldn't read the station signs fast enough and didn't know where he was or when he would even arrive.

It was a nightmare to be at his mercy like that. As soon as the conductor appeared in his carriage, Aiden looked at him expectantly, hoping for a sign from him.

But he always walked past him without paying any attention. Aiden then risked getting his backpack out of the luggage net and unpacked his packed lunch, biting hungrily into the bread, which was thickly spread with butter and honey.

Afterwards, he ate the apple and drank some water from the tin bottle, the screw cap of which was so rusty that when he unscrewed it, the reddish-brown rust fell onto his trousers.

When the train stopped once again, the conductor suddenly stood in front of him and talked at him.

Aiden looked at him uncomprehendingly.

The conductor then held up two fingers to indicate that he had two more stops before he had to get off. Aiden nodded. He hoped that he interpreted it correctly and that the train would stop twice more before he had to get off.

Again, Aiden was overcome by an immense fear of what would await him there. He felt so helpless and alone and he expected the worst. As so often before, he imagined Franz's wife would betray him immediately, and would he even be able to understand it.

She was probably standing at the station waiting for her husband to return. Full of joy and happiness to see him again.

Then she discover that this was not her husband at all, but a stranger who had taken his name and belongings and had now returned in his place, asking for her help.

Someone who doesn't even speak her language, from a hostile country and who could almost be her child.

What a shock it will be for her.

Aiden could only do one thing, and that was to give her the letter from her husband and tell her that he had sent it to her so that she would help him.

Aiden could only hope, but he could not expect anything.

It could also be the shock that Franz was no longer alive, she would send him away immediately.

Anything could happen, Aiden was aware of that.

Even if he tried to make his way on his own, he knew that he would certainly not have much of a chance, since he did not know the language, could not read anything and did not know where to go at all. He was dependent on Elisabeth's help.

But one way or another, his path would continue or end here. It was out of his hands. He remembered the words his mother often said to him and his sister:

No matter where life takes you, be sure that you are always protected and what you believe will happen. Faith has great power. Have faith in life and in yourself.

The memory of his mother's words, which had just come back to him, gave him confidence and strength and he closed his eyes, listened to himself and felt confidence again for the first time, even if only for a brief moment.

He closed his eyes and saw pictures of his mother.

He saw her standing in the field and holding out her hand to him.

Tears came out of the corners of his eyes, unstoppable, and rolled down his cheeks. He quickly wiped them away with his sleeve without opening his eyes.

*

The train braked squeakily and slowly entered a station.

When Aiden looked out of the window curiously, he saw a large construction site, around the many tracks.

Many of the other passengers got up and took their suitcases and bags out of the luggage net above the seats. It was getting noisier by the minute. Everyone was talking in confusion.

Aiden remained seated and wondered if he had now arrived in Munich? He kept a lookout for the conductor, who at that moment came hurriedly towards him and gestured impatiently with his arms.

"Boy, end of the line. You have to get off here."

He waved his hands in the air and pointed outside.

Aiden understood, rose, leaning on his crutches, and nodded his thanks to the conductor, who, however, had already turned away again and hurriedly ran into the next carriage.

Excitedly, he took his backpack with the few belongings out of the luggage net, hoisted it over his shoulder and waited until the crowd around him started moving to leave the train.

He waited until he found space to effortlessly follow the stream with his crutches towards the exit.

With difficulty he descended the two iron steps and finally stood on the platform.

He looked around with his mouth open. Many hundreds of people were milling around in the station hall, on the platforms in front of the tracks and trains.

How was he supposed to find Elisabeth here, or she him? She was expecting her husband and not him.

Indecisively, he remained standing. Again and again he was jostled by people passing by or suitcases hitting his crutches or his legs.

Many a time he groaned painfully and looked out for a place where he could stand sheltered for the time being.

He stood against one of the many concrete pillars that reached high up to the roof and supported the iron construction of the roof.

What should he do? Wait here or look for the exit from the station.

He continued to look around. The station was very large and open at the back and front. With so many people crowding in front of him, he couldn't see which way to go to get to the exit. Aiden decided to wait and see.

He observed the people around him. Those returning from the war were greeted by their families. Women and children gave shouts of joy and burst into tears.

Many of the soldiers were injured, as was Aiden. They were limping on crutches, with only one leg or arm. Some had thick bandages around their heads or an arm in a sling.

But almost everyone could see the relief on their faces and they embraced their wives and children in tears.

Standing very close to Aiden was a girl about his age.

She nervously stepped from one foot to the other.

She kept standing on tiptoe so that she could see over the crowd of people in front of her.

Aiden watched her for a while.

She had blonde hair, over which she had tied a headscarf, letting only a few cheeky curls peek out.

When she turned in his direction, he saw her face. Immediately he was fascinated by her large, blue eyes, which were accentuated particularly beautifully by the dark, thick lashes.

The look alternated between sadness and nervousness. Her fine face, whose skin seemed a little pale, was so beautiful that it took Aiden's breath away for a moment.

As her gaze lingered on him for a split second, a smile settled on her shapely lips and adorable dimples formed on her cheeks.

But the moment was quickly over, as she immediately turned her face away from him and went back to looking over the crowd.

Aiden had been standing there by the pillar for quite a while now, continuing to watch as new passengers boarded the train after a variety of farewell scenes had played out in front of him.

Those who had arrived with him slowly moved away from the platform.

Many were accompanied by their families, but there were also many who found their way to the exit on their own.

The platform emptied more and more.

Only a few people left, including the girl, that stood near him were left behind.

Aiden watched as she paced frantically back and forth, then asked one of the passing conductors something, but he just shrugged and kept walking.

Sadly, she stopped near Aiden and he watched her unobtrusively.

Reaching into his inside jacket pocket, he pulled out the letter he had received from Franz. In it was also the picture of Elisabeth that Franz had always carried with him.

He, Aiden, would recognise her if she were here. But no matter how much he looked around, he saw no woman who looked anything like the woman in the picture.

Suddenly the girl turned to him and took a step towards him and spoke to him.

"Hello, are you waiting for someone too? Did you come from the train that arrived earlier?" She looked at him expectantly.

Aiden became nervous and shrugged his shoulders.

Irritated, she looked at him.

Uncertainly, he pointed to his ears with his hand, shrugged his shoulders again to let her know that he could not hear what she was saying. He would have liked to talk to her.

The girl seemed to understand and smiled at him, whereupon those adorable dimples immediately formed on her cheeks again.

Aiden was fascinated by her laughter and would have liked to run his finger over the dimples, but refrained.

Then she suddenly pointed at herself with her index finger.

"My name is Anna! AAANNNAAA..." she repeated slowly but very loudly, as she suspected that he could hear badly or perhaps not at all, forming each letter with her lips.

Aiden understood her name. But he didn't risk repeating her name, or he might give himself away with his accent.

Pointing at himself with his finger, he said quickly: 'Franz'.

He had practised the name hundreds of times. And because it was so short and consisted of only one syllable, he could pronounce it without an accent.

The girl smiled at him again.

"So your name is Franz! Are you from here? Who are you waiting for?"

When Aiden didn't answer and just looked at her, she just kept talking.

"I understand. You can't understand me. Too bad," she said to him, but then just kept talking.

"I am waiting for my father. He was supposed to arrive on this train today. But it looks like he wasn't on it. I'm going to look around a bit more and then I'm going back home. I hope nothing else happened to him on the way home," she said sorrowfully, "I wish you all the best. Maybe we'll see each other here in Munich. Goodbye."

Anna was about to turn around when Aiden quickly grabbed her arm to stop her and held out Elisabeth's picture with his other hand.

The girl turned to him in surprise and then looked at the picture he was holding out to her.

"Who is that? Your mother?" Irritated, she looked at the picture and then at Aiden.

"Your sister?" she looked at him questioningly. But Aiden shrugged helplessly.

"You mean do I know this woman?"

She looked at the picture again more closely. Then suddenly a recognition was reflected in her features.

"Yes, she looks familiar when I look at her more closely. But I can't think right now where I know this face from?"
She stared at the picture for a moment.
"Now it comes back to me. Yes, of course, that's the wife of my former teacher, Mr von Letten. Yes, that must be her."
A smile flitted across her face.
"She also worked at the same school as her husband and I saw the two of them there together a few times. But I don't know them personally. I'm sorry. I only know that they live in Agnes Street."
Aiden didn't understand a word of what this girl was saying. Resignedly, he took the picture back, then bowed his head briefly in thanks for her help and smiled at her.
Anna felt a warm blush on her cheeks and narrowed her eyes uncertainly.
This boy was nice, even if he didn't speak a word to her. There was something about him that made a comfortable shiver run down her spine. She had never felt such a feeling before.
She liked this boy right away and wished he could talk to her. But he remained silent.
"It's a pity I can't help you. My father didn't arrive on that train either. «
She stood indecisively for a moment.
Goodbye, Franz," she finally called.
Hesitantly and smiling, she took a few steps backwards before giving him another quick wave, turning and walking away.
Aiden looked after her and thought to himself what a beautiful girl she was. If only he could talk to her, then he would run after her.

He looked after her dreamily. For a moment he forgot why he was standing here and what was waiting for him. He lost himself for a moment in this beautiful feeling.

Again he had to think of a blessing his mother had always given him:

May the boundaries you come up against leave a path open for your dreams.

She used to say to him and his sister:

Never forget your dreams and never stop dreaming, even when life is not at its best.

A smile came to his lips at the memory of his mother and her wise sayings. He loved that so much about her, even as a child.

*

When the girl had disappeared from his field of vision, he continued to look around. All the new passengers had boarded the train and the loud whistle of the steam engine announced the departure. Some windows of the train were opened and individual passengers waved once more to their families.

Aiden took his crutches and hobbled along the platform. He had to do something. He couldn't stand here all day waiting for someone who wasn't expecting him.

When he left the platform barrier and came into the waiting area of the station, he first sat down on a bench. He took the water bottle out of his canvas bag and drank the last sips of water. Unfortunately, he had nothing left to eat.

There were only a few coins left in his pocket, which Sister Jutta had slipped him.

What was he supposed to do now? Aiden didn't know where to go.

He hadn't thought about what would happen beforehand if Elisabeth didn't show up. No, he had simply been too afraid to think about it.

Again he looked around. After a while, he stood up and walked towards the exit.

He felt more helpless by the minute. He had the address of Elisabeth's home, but he couldn't ask anyone.

When he stepped out of the large swinging door in front of the station building on the station square, he first stopped, surprised at what he saw there. The large square in front of the station was bustling with traffic. Cars were parked in front of the car park, the likes of which Aiden had never seen before.

On his journey to the front in France, he saw many a car driving from the train.

And in Heidelberg, as he was being taken through the city to the train station, he saw individual automobiles in various designs.

But there were at least twenty of them parked here, if not more. And there were also many cars on the streets.

In between, every now and then, a horse-drawn carriage drove by, but the automobiles were in the majority.

Aiden watched this hustle and bustle for a while, fascinated, until he heard a loud jingling sound. A strange vehicle, similar to a small train, approached from the right, running on rails anchored between the cobblestones.

There were wires stretched over the vehicle, with which the vehicle was connected to a pole.

Aiden had never seen anything like it. His parents had told him that for a few years there had been a trams in the city, in Dublin.

His father had fascinated him and described exactly how this vehicle was electrically powered.

But Aiden could not imagine much about it.

And now he stood here thinking that this was surely one of those trams his father had told him about.

It was already very late, as Aiden could see on a large clock attached to the station building. The clock pointed to eight.

Indecisively he stood there, leaning on his crutches, tired from the long journey, desperate and hungry.

Carefully, he hobbled along on his crutches when a horse-drawn carriage stopped in front of him.

"Well, boy, shall I take you somewhere?" the coachman called out to him.

Aiden looked up at him and shrugged his shoulders. He pointed to his ears so that he understood that he couldn't hear anything.

Then he had an idea.

He reached into his jacket pocket and took out the letter written by Franz and addressed to Elisabeth and showed the coachman the address.

After looking at the letter, the coachman nodded his head thoughtfully.

"I can take you there, boy. Do you have any money?" he looked eagerly at Aiden. When he didn't respond, he rubbed the thumb and forefinger of his right hand together to indicate to Aiden what he wanted.

Aiden also understood this movement immediately and

reached into his jacket pocket, which contained the individual coins Sister Jutta had slipped him.

Aiden had no idea how much it was and whether it would be enough for the ride. With his palm open, he held the coins out to the driver.

The latter looked at Aiden's hand and frowned.

"Well, it's not much. But because you have served your country so faithfully, I don't want to be like that. "and climbed down from his carriage seat.

The coachman took the coins from Aiden's palm and slipped them into his trouser pocket.

"Well, here we go. It will be best if you sit in the back of the truck.

Climbing onto the coach box will be too high for you with your injured leg. It's more comfortable for you back here," and he tapped the wood of the loading area with his hand.

Aiden let everything happen to him and hoped that he was taken to the right place.

The coachman got back on his coach box and took the reins in his hands and spurred his horse on.

Aiden looked around with interest under the ride. They drove past beautiful, magnificent buildings.

The war had hardly left any traces here in this city.

Nothing to see of the battlefield that was marked by destruction and death.

As he was to learn later, the city of Munich had been spared attacks and no major damage had been done.

Aiden saw men in worn suits or work clothes and women, some with fancy dresses and hats on their heads or with worn servants' clothes, Aiden guessed.

He marvelled at this hustle and bustle on the streets and kept looking behind a passing automobile that he had never seen before.

Suddenly he was thrown quite roughly against the wooden wall of the cart when the coachman forced his horses to stop sharply.

"Brrrrr! Brrrrrrr!" the coachman roared loudly "Stop! Brrrrrr."

Only with great difficulty and at the very last moment was he able to bring the horses and thus the vehicle to a halt.

It wouldn't have taken much for the coachman to drive straight into a tram coming up from the side. The horses shied because of the loud noise and the coachman had a hard time calming them down.

When the tram had passed, the horses calmed down again and the journey could continue. But not without the coachman swearing loudly after the tram.

Aiden could not understand anything, but he could guess from the tone of voice that the coachman had not said anything friendly.

A small smile flitted across his face.

He thought of his father, who reacted in a similarly hot-tempered way when he found himself in situations that were actually his fault, but which he definitely did not want to admit.

The coachman calmed down again after a while and the journey through the city continued.

After what felt like an eternity, the coachman turned to Aiden.

"We'll be in Agnes Street in a minute. What number do you have to go to?" he looked at Aiden questioningly.

The latter could not even guess what the coachman wanted from him.

"What house number?" the latter called out again impatiently.

Aiden looked at the coachman, disturbed. The coachman raised his eyebrows in annoyance, but then indicated with his hands that he wanted to see the letter again.

When he understood, he handed him the letter with relief.

After reading the house number 11, he handed the letter back to Aiden, who put it safely back in the inside pocket of his jacket.

After another five minutes, the coachman turned into a road lined left and right with half-high trees.

Behind them were beautifully decorated multi-storey houses, some with paintings on the walls or elaborate balconies built on concrete pillars.

The coachman stopped in front of one of these houses, turned back to Aiden and pointed to a large, heavy, double-leaf wooden door that seemed to lead into the house he wanted to go into.

Nodding gratefully, he grabbed his sack and wooden crutches and crawled off the truck bed on his backside.

As soon as he stood on the pavement, the coachman set his horses in motion again, still waving him with one hand, but without looking back at him.

Aiden stood there and looked around. Everything seemed so clean. The street and also the pavement, the houses, the individual people who walked past him without paying attention to him, were so very different from what he was used to at home, in Ireland.

Perplexed, he looked up at the façade of the house.

What should he do now?

He looked at the large wooden door and walked towards it.

Next to the door was a large metal 11.

Aiden took out the letter and saw the same number there, on the letter.

Carefully, he pushed against the door, which burst open with a loud creak.

Cautiously, he looked through the gap of the open door into the dark hallway.

He could not make out much. Suddenly the door was ripped open even wider from inside.

Aiden was so frightened that he almost fell over if he hadn't caught himself with his crutches at the last moment.

A small boy stood in front of him with a very deranged looking ball in his hand. The boy looked at him questioningly. He must be eight or ten years old at the most, Aiden thought.

"Do you want to come in here?" the boy asked curiously "My name is Karl and what is yours?"

"Franz.", Aiden answered quickly.

Then he quickly showed him the letter he still had in his hands with the address of Elisabeth von Letten.

"You want to see Elisabeth. Yes, she lives upstairs on the second floor" and pointed upwards at his words and he slipped past him and ran out into the street.

Aiden glanced after him briefly before stepping through the door that led into a beige, blue-tiled hallway.

There, a wide, brown wooden staircase wound its way upwards, snail-like, as he could see from below through the staircase eye.

Fascinated, he looked at the banister. The handrail was made of wood, mounted on forged iron rose vines painted lime green and red.

He couldn't help but be amazed. How magnificent the houses were here. Outside as well as inside.

He held on to the banister with one hand and supported himself on his crutches with the other as he slowly limped up the wooden stairs.

When he reached the first floor, he saw three doors, each with a gold-coloured iron plate with a name on it. He pulled out the letter again and compared the names. But he could not decipher the name 'von Letten'.

So he went on to the next floor. When he arrived there, breathing heavily, he saw that there were again three entrance doors, just like one floor below, with the golden name plates. This time he was lucky and read the name he was looking for on the second door.

There was a bell on the wall to the right. He still hesitated to press it. He took a deep breath and thought about what he should say.

A thousand times he had thought about how he would begin when he faced her. But never did his words seem appropriate.

Was Elisabeth there at all? Why hadn't she been at the station? Had he simply not seen her and she had left again? Was she already at home or still on the way? No matter how many questions he asked himself, he couldn't answer them himself.

After another brief hesitation, he mustered all his courage and pressed the bell.

*

After the third ring, which again went unheard and the door was not opened, Aiden wondered what he should do.

Exhausted, he sat down on the stairs that led further up to the next floor. He leaned his head against the wall. He wanted to rest a little. Should he wait? She had to show up sometime. Where else was he supposed to go?

He closed his eyes. He was so tired after the long journey and all the excitement.

Briefly, the image of the beautiful girl came to his mind. What was her name again? Anna, yes, Anna was her name and a smile came over his face when he thought of her.

With this thought, he slipped into a sleep and a dream revealed itself.

With Anna by his hand, he roamed the lush green meadows of his native Ireland. Chasing the sheep that had strayed too far from their pasture. Happily he lay with her in the grass, under a tree, and Aiden told her the story of the wishing tree under which the fairies lived, and anyone who made a wish under this tree was immediately granted it by the fairies. Anna laughed radiantly at his words and whispered something to the tree.

Aiden asked her what she had said and looked at her expectantly.

"That I want to be kissed by a boy named Aiden now," she confessed to him, her cheeks flushing.

Aiden leaned towards her and approached her lips.

*

"Hello, isn't Elisabeth at home? "a child's voice called out and pulled him out of his dream.

Aiden opened his eyes. Still caught up in his dream and full of anticipation for the kiss he was about to give Anna.

But disappointed, he only saw the boy from earlier standing next to him, grinning and curious.

He shook his head briefly to wake up properly. The boy was playing around with his ball in front of Aiden and chatting away.

"It's possible that she's not there. Then she'll be out and about in the city. You know, she's raising money for a new school from the rich people downtown. And looking for a new building. The old school was closed down and turned into a military hospital. But you know," he continued, now with a mischievous grin on his face, "I didn't mind at all that the school was closed. For weeks we had to cancel classes because there were no substitute rooms so quickly."

Chuckling, he held a hand in front of his mouth to keep from laughing out loud.

Aiden didn't understand a word of what the boy was saying, except for a few words he had heard before. But it was not enough to make any sense of it. Again he was very annoyed that he could not understand anything.

The boy suddenly stopped chattering and made his way up the stairs to the next floor.

"If you don't want to talk to me, then I'll leave. Goodbye," he shouted when he received no reply from Aiden and he was gone, swallowed up by the winding staircase that snaked elegantly upwards.

Aiden remained seated.

How much time had passed since he had fallen asleep here? High up in the stairwell was a window through which he could see outside.

It was already dark, so he must have been asleep for a while.

133

Unfortunately, he didn't have a watch to tell the exact time and was wondering whether he should go out again. But where to?

At that moment he heard the clatter of the door downstairs and footsteps on the stairs.

Tensely, he remained sitting on the landing. He straightened up a little so that he could catch a glimpse of the person coming up through the eye of the stairs. It was a woman with brown, short-cropped hair, he could already see that.

As she climbed the last landing, head bowed, one hand rummaging in her coat pocket, Aiden held his breath in excitement. Was that her? Was that Elisabeth?

The woman reached the second floor and finally pulled the key out of her coat pocket and walked towards the flat door with the name tag 'von Letten'.

At that moment she noticed Aiden and took a step back, startled.

'Who is he? What does he want here? Is he waiting for me?' she looked suspiciously at Aiden.

The latter stood up awkwardly. Elisabeth defensively took another step back.

Aiden reached into his jacket pocket and pulled out the letter and held it out to Elizabeth.

Still he did not say a word. He was afraid of her reaction if he spoke to her in English.

Elisabeth stared at the letter, then back at Aiden, but made no move to reach for it.

"Franz!" whispered Aiden meekly.

Elisabeth's face showed surprise mixed with fear and suspicion.

"Is the letter from Franz?" she asked softly. "Where is he? He was supposed to come home today. I went to the station but I didn't find him?"

Aiden looked at her and tears came to his eyes. He had to tell her that her husband was dead and that he had come in his place.

He was incredibly afraid of it.

Maybe she would start screaming immediately and the other inhabitants of the house would become aware of him. Then it had all been for nothing.

The woman was still suspicious of him. Aiden still held the letter out to her.

Elisabeth looked into his face and eyed him. Aiden also looked at Elisabeth more closely.

Her hands were in black, thin leather gloves. He saw her beige knee-length coat held around her waist with a black belt. Under the coat, a long brown skirt reached to her ankles. Her feet were in black, sturdy shoes. Her brown, short-cropped hair, which she had combed out. Her beautiful face, with its fine features, made her look very young. Her large brown eyes were wrinkled with sorrow and sadness marked her gaze.

After what felt like an eternity, Elisabeth took a step towards Aiden and took the letter from his hand.

When she glanced at it, tears immediately came to her eyes and rolled down her cheeks.

"What about Franz?" she whispered in a voice filled with fear.

Aiden understood what she said and wanted to know. And now it was up to him to say the words.

"Franz dead.", he whispers tonelessly, choked by his rising tears.

Elizabeth looked at him in disbelief and at that moment froze in total defensiveness towards Aiden.

"What are you saying? How do you know that? Who are you anyway? What is your name? Where did you get the letter?" she shouted in an angry voice.

Aiden knew that now he had to come forward. He had to make himself known and speak to her in his own language so that he could explain everything to her.

They were still standing in the stairwell. Elisabeth with the flat key in one hand and the letter in the other. But she made no effort to unlock the flat door.

"Aiden my name," he said in a heavy accent. He anxiously tried to gauge her reaction.

Elisabeth looked at him in irritation. Fear rose up in her. She thought she had misheard him. What had the boy just said? And especially how he had pronounced it.

"Sorry. Please do not be afraid of me. I am Irish and a friend of Franz."

Elisabeth froze and opened her mouth as if she was about to scream.

But she wordlessly closed her mouth again, turned abruptly, hastily inserted the key into the lock of the flat door, unlocked it, slipped hastily in and
slammed it shut from the inside and locked it.

Aiden stared at the flat door, on the one hand relieved that she hadn't yelled the whole house together, but also despondent about what to do now.

Where should he spend the night tonight if she wouldn't take him in. And it looked like she didn't want to have anything to do with him.

Despondent, he sat back down on the steps.

Thirst and hunger overwhelmed him, but he had no more coins and no idea where to sleep.

Should he try again and ring Elisabeth's doorbell? But he suspected that she would not open the door for him. She surely had to process all this first.

Despondently, he lowered his hand again, which he had already raised to the bell.

Suddenly he heard voices and a door slam, high above him in the stairwell.

Anxiously, he grabbed his crutches and limped down the stairs as fast as he could.

When he arrived on the ground floor, in front of the large front door, he looked around and discovered a niche under the stairs where a door was hidden.

He quickly ducked into the alcove and pushed against the door, which immediately burst open. Behind it was a small room that probably served as a storeroom.

Through a small, barred window facing the street, a little light from the streetlamp filtered into the room.

Although it was very dark, Aiden could see all kinds of junk, like old wooden boxes and small, broken children's bicycles. There was some coal stored in one corner and several sacks and old blankets in the opposite corner.

He quickly stepped into the narrow room, bent over, and closed the door behind him as quietly as possible, as he could already hear the footsteps and voices of the people who had now reached the ground floor and were stepping out into the open, talking loudly.

Aiden breathed a sigh of relief.

Should he spend his night here and ring Elisabeth's doorbell again tomorrow? What else could he do? Night was already falling.

Stooping, he hobbled to the corner where the sacks and blankets were stored, spread and stacked the sacks on the floor and put the thick, grey and dusty blankets over them.

It was very stuffy in this small room, but it had the advantage that the temperature was relatively pleasant and the night might not be quite so cold.

The October nights could already be very rough.

Before settling down on his makeshift bed, he looked around the room. Also in the hope of perhaps finding something to eat or drink somewhere. Unfortunately, his hope was not fulfilled.

For a while, he looked through the small, barred window at the pavement lit by the streetlamp and down the street to the house opposite.

Only a few people were on the road.

Aiden could only assume that it was now later in the evening than he had suspected.

After he had settled down on his campbed, he unpacked his tin bottle and was able to drink one last small sip of water from it. This was only enough to moisten his mouth, which was already very dry.

Tomorrow he had to set out to perhaps find a well, with drinkable water.

Aiden tried not to panic and forced himself to think calmly about what he would do next.

He did not have many opportunities.

Resigned and desperate, he thought about just lying here in the room, closing his eyes, sleeping and never getting up again and ending this nightmare.

Aiden put the backpack with his belongings under his head, reached into his pocket and took out the golden coin.

Firmly he held the coin in his palm and hoped for an answer. What could he do? He couldn't just give up like that, could he? He had come so far now and had arrived here in Munich. But how was he supposed to make it without Elisabeth's help?

The biggest problem was that he could not speak or understand anything. This hurdle seemed so insurmountable that he sobbed and crossed his arms over his face in despair and began to cry bitterly.

But exhausted by the long day and his despair, his eyelids slowly became heavy and at last he slipped into a relieving sleep, which, however, was marked by confused dreams that kept bringing him out of the sleep and startled him. Each time he looked out of the window to see if it would soon be light, but the night dragged on endlessly.

Thirst and hunger did their bit to make the night drag on for an agonisingly long time.

At some point, when he was again startled out of sleep, he saw through the small window that the morning was slowly dawning.

Suddenly he noticed that he was still holding the golden coin tightly in his hand

With difficulty, he stood up with the help of his crutches, stowed the golden coin safely in his jacket, took his backpack and went to the door.

He urgently needed to get out into the open.

Cautiously, he opened the small door that led into the tiled entrance to the house. Everything was quiet in the house.

Carefully, he slipped through the door and went to the large entrance door, which opened easily from the inside.

Aiden inspected the door briefly and saw that there was only one button on the outside, which meant he could not simply open the door from the outside. He thought hard about how the door had opened yesterday when he had arrived. He could not remember. He was too exhausted yesterday. Had it been open?

Then it came back to him. The boy with the ball had just come out and left the door open for him.

What should he do now? If the door closed behind him, he couldn't get back into the house. He looked around and discovered a red toy car carved out of wood in a corner of the hallway.

He quickly fetched it from the corner and placed it in the door frame so that the front door could not close while he was outside.

He hurriedly stepped out into the open, quickly went to the nearest tree and relieved himself.

Outside on the pavement, he looked around. There was not a soul in sight. Only at the end of the road a wooden cart pulled by two horses was passing.

Indecisively, he stepped back onto the pavement again and made sure that the toy car was still holding the front door open.

Desperately, he searched the street for a well. But he did not find one.

He walked one more block. However, he did not want to go too far away from the house, for fear that he might not find his way back.

He had no luck. Not a well to be seen for miles around. It was still very early in the morning, but slowly the city was waking up.

Many lights were already burning behind the windows and life was also awakening on the street.

Aiden went back to house number 11. He took the toy car and put it back in the corner of the hallway and closed the door from the inside. Then he stood there and thought about what to do.

Before he could make a decision, he heard voices and footsteps on the stairs, approaching from above. He quickly wanted to hide in the alcove behind the stairs.

In his haste, he tripped over one of his crutches and fell onto the hard stone tiles, unable to prevent a loud cry.

The voices that could be heard from the stairs fell silent for a moment before the two people hurried down the last steps to see where the outcry was coming from.

There were two women, one of them Elisabeth, Aiden was startled to realise as he lifted his head, just trying to stand up again. Elisabeth rushed towards him and grabbed him by the elbow and pulled him up.

"Are you still here?" she exclaimed in amazement, looking at him reproachfully out of her very swollen and reddened eyes. "What are you still doing here?"

Aiden looked at her when he finally stood up straight in front of her. She looked terrible. Her face puffy, tired and her eyes red from crying.

"Who's that?" asked the other woman, dressed in a grey female uniform, eyeing Aiden suspiciously.

"This boy came to my door yesterday and delivered Franz's letter," Elisabeth explained to her friend, looking at Aiden. "I don't know how he knows him. He doesn't speak to me." Elisabeth did not mention that the boy had spoken to her in English yesterday.

*

After closing the door in the boy's face last night, she had gone into the kitchen as if in a trance and first sat down and looked at the letter.

She no longer understood anything at all.

Franz had not arrived in Munich by train yesterday as announced. This was already upsetting enough for Elisabeth. She was looking forward to finally see her husband again. She had prepared a small feast for them both and even managed to get hold of a bottle of wine. Even if it was cheap fluff, it was something special in these times.

She had baked bread and stewed vegetables with a small piece of meat. She had been on the road for a day to find this piece of meat in Munich.

The supply was getting worse by the week. And her money reserves were also slowly running out. She had to manage it well.

Yesterday, however, she had not hesitated and bought a piece of meat from a black marketeer. For his homecoming, she wanted to offer him something special.

The food was getting cold on the cooker, the bottle of wine was open on the table, which was set with two plates and two glasses.

142

And now she was sitting there with the letter in her hand. Great fear seized her, she stared at it and could not open it. Who was this boy, who seemed to be English? How did he get here, in his German uniform, with the letter from Franz? Elisabeth began to tremble.

She sensed that something must have happened.

She had had this feeling for some time, since there was no more mail from Franz, but she kept repressing it.

Every day she went to the military hospital, where she also worked by the hour, helping the nurses as much as possible since the school where she had worked had been turned into a military hospital.

The current lists with the reported dead and missing were also hung there.

Franz's name was not among them, which was a great relief to Elisabeth. But on the other hand, she had not received a letter from him for almost three months now, which again made her very anxious.

They kept blaming it on the fact that the forwarding of field mail had certainly been stopped. However, they did not get any information about this.

After she had calmed down a little, she forced herself to open the letter.

Even at the first words, tears ran down her cheeks.

My beloved Elisabeth,

When you hold this letter in your hands, I am already up there in the kingdom of heaven looking at you. I firmly believe that the Kingdom of Heaven exists and that we will all get there one day and we will meet again.

Only yesterday an officer who was badly hit said in my arms just before he died ' I am no longer afraid. We are all going up to the kingdom of heaven, because we have already had hell here on earth.

I know it will be very hard for you and that you will be infinitely sad. But remember what a wonderful time we had together before this cruel war began. No one can take this time away from us and I will take it with me to my heavenly kingdom. And one day we will meet again, I am sure of it.

Now I have to say goodbye to you. I wish our dream of having our own child had come true. Then you wouldn't be alone and you would have someone to give you strength.

But it was not meant to be and was not foreseen in our life together. Instead, we had our school children, who brought us much joy and whom we were able to learn a lot from, and you can still do so. I have heard that our school has been closed. I hope so much that there will be a new school and that you can continue to teach and be with your children.

I am sure you will manage to live a good life even without me. I want to tell you one more thing: I loved you very much and I still do and I always will. You are a great woman. I could never have wished for anyone better.

Thank you for your love that will never end and everything you have done for me and all the best for your Future, hopefully still long, happy life.

Your ever-loving Franz

PS: Always listen to your heart, because it is pure and you will always go the right way.

Elisabeth sat in the kitchen for a long time with the letter in her hand and cried.

At some point, after she had recovered from the initial shock she got up and went to the flat door, unlocked it and looked out into the hallway to see if the young man was still there. But he had disappeared.

She was sorry that she had simply slammed the door in his face.

Now she would have liked to talk to him and find out where he got the letter and whether he knew Franz.

Franz had not mentioned this young man in his letter.

So he only met him after he had written the letter. Or the boy found Franz dead and stole the letter from him and they didn't know each other at all.

Again, she thought, Franz knew the English language and therefore it was quite possible that the two had spoken to each other.

It was clear to Elisabeth that he was an enemy in German uniform. But she did not have the feeling that he wanted to harm her. He seemed very scared himself and was still very, very young.

No matter how much she thought about it, she couldn't find an explanation. Until the thought occurred to her whether it was perhaps possible that Franz had sent him to her? But this possibility seemed too absurd to her.

But still the thought did not let her go. Franz had a very big heart and Elisabeth was sure that he would not have closed it even to the enemy.

Now it was too late to find out, because the boy was gone and she would probably never meet him again.

Now she had to live with this uncertainty.

Maybe the boy could have told her something else about Franz. About his last words and what exactly had happened to him.

Tears ran down her face again as she thought about what Franz must have gone through.

She spent the next few hours reading the letter over and over again, just sitting there, remembering their time together and mourning it with her tears.

In the process, she emptied half the bottle of wine and the unaccustomed consumption of alcohol helped her to fall into a restless but relieving sleep.

*

Now this boy, here in the stairwell, stood before her again. Her compassionate heart stirred within her, as did curiosity as to what this boy was all about.

"Greta, you go ahead to the hospital. I'll take care of the boy for now. I'll join you later."

Greta looked at her in horror.

"What do you want from him. Just be careful. It's not that he's out to rob you. You don't know where he got the letter from Franz and whether he's not just trying to sneak into your house. Be careful," Greta eyed Aiden suspiciously.

"I'll take care of myself Greta. Don't worry."

Meanwhile, the two women were talking and seemingly talking about him, Aiden noticed his knees starting to buckle. to tremble. He was so incredibly thirsty and a weakness overcame him that he had to quickly lean against the wall to prevent himself from falling over.

Elisabeth noticed this and supported him by putting his arm around her shoulder and wrapping her arm around his lean waist.

Greta was still standing on the stairs, shaking her head. She could not understand Elisabeth's naivety. In those times, no one could be trusted and everyone had to protect themselves as best they could. Especially they, as women, were easy victims for the men who had become raw through the war.

Never would she have had the willingness, like Elisabeth, to help this stranger, of whom she knew nothing except that he had a letter from Franz with him.

Greta had been friends with Elisabeth and Franz for several years, since she had moved into the third-floor flat with her aunt five years ago, to be exact.

The aunt had died a year ago and since then she had lived alone in the flat.

Greta was 38 years old, had her ash-blonde hair combed tightly back into a knot. Her ice-blue eyes looked mostly forbidding from her gaunt, pale face.

Only when she was alone with Elisabeth did she take off this mask and she became a little softer in her posture.

Until the beginning of the war, she was employed as a nanny in a rich household.

However, the family fled to the countryside shortly after the war began, leaving Greta without a job.

Since then, she also helped out in the military hospital and lived off the
savings that her aunt had left her.

Elisabeth had never seen a man at Greta's side during this time and she did not inquire further because Greta was very secretive about this.

"Do what you have to do," Greta finally cried. "But I warned you. Be careful."

With that, she adjusted her little grey hat and rushed away through the front door.

Elisabeth looked after her and then turned back to Aiden, who was still leaning against the wall, supported by Elisabeth.

"You come with me to the flat for now. Then we'll see what happens.

Aiden looked at her uncertainly. He could not understand what she had said.

"Come on Boy, let's go up.", Elisabeth said to him quietly with her broken English, pulling him towards the stairs.

The boy was so thin and emaciated that it was not too difficult for Elisabeth to support him. But without his help, she would not manage to get him up the stairs.

Aiden now understood that she wanted to take him back to the flat with her. He was so grateful to hear a few words in his language.

He felt so exhausted that he had almost no strength left to hold himself up. But he knew he had to muster all his remaining strength.

He dropped the crutches to the floor and held on to the banister with his right hand.

He was already able to put some weight on his foot again and could take help. Elisabeth supported him on his left side. Slowly and with great effort, they made it up the first flight of stairs and arrived on the first floor. There they paused for a moment to regain their strength. Aiden's face was dripping with sweat as he summoned up the last of his strength.

Elisabeth's arms were already shaking from the effort she was putting into supporting Aiden.

"Your name is Aiden?" she assured herself, breathing heavily, and looked at him.

"Yes.", he answered in German and couldn't help smiling briefly at the curiosity of their togetherness.

"Come on," Elisabeth urged him on.

And once again they set out to conquer the next set of stairs. After another pause, they made it up the last flight of stairs and finally stood in front of the flat door. Elisabeth unlocked it and Aiden hobbled into the hallway of the flat. Elisabeth quickly ran down the stairs and fetched the crutches. Then she quickly locked the flat door.

Aiden could barely stay on his feet.

From the hallway, a door led into a large room, into which Elisabeth now continued to support him and finally sat him down on a large sofa covered in red-green fabric with a floral pattern.

Breathing heavily, Aiden dropped into the cushion and closed his eyes. He was at the end of his tether.

"Water.", he whispered powerlessly.

Elisabeth hurriedly ran into the adjoining small kitchen and fetched a glass of water. When she returned to the living room, Aiden was sitting there with his eyes closed and Elisabeth thought he had fallen asleep.

But he had to drink first, so she shook his arm and he opened his eyes.

Elisabeth handed him the glass of water. Aiden reached for it, but was shaking so much that he spilled most of it. So Elisabeth helped him and held the glass to his lips. Greedily, Aiden drank it down in one gulp.

"More, please." He looked at Elisabeth pleadingly.

The latter immediately went back to the kitchen and came back again with a filled glass, which he again drank down to the last drop and then let himself fall back exhausted on the sofa and closed his eyes, instantly falling asleep.

Elisabeth stood in front of him and looked at him for a while.

He was still so young, she thought, and compassion stirred in her. Poor boy. Where was his home? And how did he get here?

Many questions preoccupied her. She took off his shoes as gently as possible so that he would not wake up.

Dressed as he was, she pressed him gently onto the sofa cushion, lifted his feet up and bedded him down on the sofa. Then she fetched a woollen blanket from the bedroom and covered him.

He will probably sleep for a while, she thought. But she absolutely had to go to the military hospital and let them know that she couldn't come for the next few days because she had received the terrible news that her husband had been killed. Everyone at the military hospital would understand.

But could she leave this boy here alone in the flat? Two voices were fighting inside her. Could she trust him? What if she came back and he was no longer here, gone with the few belongings she had that he could take with him to turn into money?

Carefully, she undid the buttons of his grey jacket and scanned the inside pockets to see if he had a weapon on him. But here she found nothing except a big round hard thing stuck in one of the inside pockets. When she reached in, she felt metal and pulled it out.

What she saw there amazed her. She held a golden coin in her hand that was much bigger than the coinage she knew. When she looked at the coin more closely, she could see writing on it in a language she did not know. She could only decipher one word and that was 'Eire'. But she did not know what it meant.

Elisabeth wondered very much why the boy was carrying such a coin, which looked very valuable.

Yes, there were many questions she had to ask him. Hopefully her knowledge of English was enough to understand him and be able to talk to him.

She quickly put the coin back in his pocket and stepped up to her lavishly stocked bookshelf.

Franz and she always loved books and read a lot. Elisabeth knew that Franz had a thick notebook that he had once received from his father.

There were a lot of translations from German to English in it.

Franz's father was a diplomat, travelled a lot to other countries and knew the English language, which he had taught his son very early. And Franz had taught it to her.

It had been a while and Elisabeth had trouble remembering all the words.

At the beginning of their marriage, they spent days speaking only English to each other. This was the best way, Franz said, to learn the language. And even though Elisabeth never mastered the language perfectly, she could communicate well.

However, in recent years, especially since Franz had to go to war, she had hardly spoken English.

Now the fact that she knew Franz had been able to communicate with the boy kept her from rejecting him. First she wanted to find out what exactly had happened. How he had got the letter and why he had travelled here.

How could he smuggle himself into Germany as an enemy without being exposed? Questions upon questions flooded Elisabeth's mind.

She briefly leafed through the notebook, which listed words and phrases in neat handwriting, which were then translated into English, written down.

She would read that over again later. First she had to go to the military hospital.

She looked at Aiden, who still seemed to be sound asleep and not stirring.

Elisabeth listened within herself for a moment, to her inner voice, whether she

could leave him here alone.

Her mind alone fuelled these fears and doubts, but now she pushed them away. She knew instinctively that this was not a bad boy.

She quickly fetched a piece of paper and a pen and wrote him another note saying she would see him later, hoping he could read it. She placed the note in front of him on the small dark brown living room table.

On the dining table next to the sofa, she placed a plate with bread and a piece of cheese, as well as a full jug of water.

She thought he would understand that this was meant for him.

After one last look at Aiden, she hurriedly left the flat and locked it from the outside. She had no other option, as she could not leave the flat door open.

Too many burglars and looters were out and about and would stop at nothing.

She hoped Aiden wouldn't panic when he noticed the flat door was locked.

She quickly made her way, tot he hospital. Only now did tears come again as she hurried down the stairs to the entrance of the house and she realised again the finality that Franz would never return to her.

She wanted to ask the nurses to give her some time off.

They would be lenient and grant her the days off because she was not a permanent employee but only temporarily employed there.

*

Aiden could only open his eyes with difficulty as he awoke from a deep sleep of exhaustion.

At first he did not know where he was. He perceived the sofa on which he was lying, then slowly his memory came back.

Elisabeth had taken him into the flat. She had given him water to drink, then he could remember nothing more. He must have fallen asleep immediately. Tired, he straightened up and put his feet with the grey woollen socks on the flowered carpet. Elisabeth had taken his shoes off, because he couldn't remember doing it himself.

He was tormented by an indescribable thirst. His mouth was parched and he looked around. He noticed the note in front of him on the low living room table and took it in his hand. See you later, the note said in English script. Had she gone away?

"Hello!" he called cautiously.

But he got no answer, which led him to conclude that he was alone in the flat.

Looking around further, he saw the carafe of water on the dining table and a glass. He stood up and poured himself water and greedily drank two glasses empty.

Then he noticed the bread and cheese, on the plate provided. Was this supposed to be for him? His stomach growled loudly as he looked at the food.

He sat down on the chair and took the bread and cheese, assuming it was meant for him, and greedily devoured it all in no time.

Elisabeth really seemed to be a very good person, Aiden thought. Just like Franz had told him there on the battlefield, and she could speak his language, too.

But there was still no certainty for him that she would help him. Maybe she just called the police and had them pick him up?

Fear flooded through him at the thought.

Aiden remained sitting at the dining table for a while, looking around.

The room was simply furnished. The dark wooden floor was covered extensively with carpets. The walls were painted in an old pink colour and made the room appear bright and friendly.

Against one wall was a small dark brown living room cupboard with a glass case containing some glasses and a coffee service.

On the other wall, to the right of the cupboard, was the sofa on which he had slept. In front of it was a small, low wooden table and another armchair covered in lime green fabric.

But what attracted Aiden's attention the most was the wall shelf that almost completely filled the whole wall with books. He stood up and limped to the shelf.

As he stood in front of the books, he let his gaze wander slowly over the spines. Although he had never owned books at home before and his parents didn't own many books either, he was fascinated by them.

*

His parents had a Bible at home. Often, when he was twelve or thirteen years old, he would pick up the book and leaf through it. He had never read it directly, but that was because he had tried, but had not really understood anything that was in the book.

Once he had asked his mother if she could explain to him what these strange verses meant, but she waved them off and told him that it was enough if he listened to the words of the priest in church, because he proclaimed exactly what was in the Bible.

At that time, Aiden did not know that the priest proclaimed the Word of God, i.e. the words from the Bible, but that each priest passed this on in his own interpretation.

As Aiden looked at the books, letting his mind wander to his childhood home, a leaden heaviness settled on his chest.

He quickly pushed them aside and continued to look at the books. He could read the writing on the spines, but the words were foreign to him.

Then he discovered a book with the name 'Oscar Wilde' on the spine. He had heard this name before, he thought frantically.

Aiden carefully pulled the book from the shelf and looked at the title. Then a memory surfaced in him.

His mother had read him and his sister Eimear a story one evening.

This did not happen often, rather she mostly told freely invented stories and legends.

But a friend in the village had given her the book 'The Canterville Ghost' for her children, because she no longer wanted it in her household, as the author Oscar Wilde was dead and had not left the best reputation.

Aiden's mother Eileen had first read the book herself and enjoyed it so much that she wanted to read it to her children. They sat in front of the fireplace in their little cottage. Aiden snuggled tightly against his mother and Eimear on the other side in her mother's arms. She told them that the author was also Irish and came from Dublin.

They listened intently to the story and many times Aiden was frightened by the stories about the ghost, but many times they laughed together at the funny scenes.

Later, her father joined her and sat down in his armchair, listening with amusement.

This was one of the many evenings that Aiden remembers particularly fondly. Because most of the time his mother was tired and exhausted from the hard, heavy work and didn't have much time for musical hours.

But despite this, she gave them attention and love as much as she could and the two siblings always felt that they were loved.

*

Aiden looked at the book in his hand for some time, engrossed in his memories, before opening it. It was in English, he was pleased to see.

He sat down with it on the sofa and began to read.

'When Mr. Hiram B. Otis, the American envoy, bought Canterville Castle, everyone told him he was doing very foolishly, as that castle was undoubtedly cursed......'

After a few chapters, Aiden's eyes fell closed and he fell asleep with the book in his hand and a smile on his face.

*

When Elisabeth returned from the hospital a few hours later, she found the boy sitting on the sofa asleep with a book in his hand.

She took off her coat and hung it over the armchair. She let her gaze wander to the dining table and saw that everything she had provided for him had been eaten.

Carefully, she took the book from his hands. At that moment he opened his eyes and was startled to see Elisabeth standing right in front of him.

"Do you know the book?" she asked him.

"Yes.", he replied. "My mother read it to me once when I was little."

Confused, she looked at him. She found it a little difficult to understand his strange accent.

"You have to speak slower or I won't understand you."

Aiden then repeated his words slowly, striving for a more understandable pronunciation.

He already had problems at the front, with his English comrades, sometimes, that they understood him and the Irish in general.

While it was the same language, the Irish was still very much influenced by the old Gaelic language of Ireland.

Aiden's father almost invariably spoke Gaelic to his children, while their mother spoke Gaelic to him and his sister, but mainly always spoke in English.

"Where are you from?" she asked Aiden.

"I'm Irish. I live not too far from Dublin, near the village of Tara, just below the Hill of Tara."

"Oh, that's why you know this book by Oscar Wilde, who was also Irish," Elisabeth speculated, letting her gaze glide over the book.

"Do you want to tell me how you got the letter that Franz wrote for me? And why you came here in his place?" she looked at him expectantly, but also fearfully, her eyes heavy with tears. "But maybe you should take a bath first. I think you need it. Then I'll make us some coffee and you can tell me everything I need to know calmly afterwards."

With a sorrowful face, she turned away, put the book on the living room table and went into one of the adjoining rooms. When she came back, she had clothes and a towel in her hand.

"These are Franz's clothes. They're probably too big for you, but they're better than the dirty ones you're wearing now. I'll wash them and in a day or two you can have them back."

She went ahead and opened another door and showed him the bathroom.

"I'll heat up some water. In the meantime you can shave.

It's not much beard sprouting on your face, but it looks unkempt," pointing at his face and leaving the bathroom.

Aiden had to grin despite the difficult situation. His mother had often said the same thing to him.

He stepped up to the small mirror that hung above a round wash tub.

Curiously, he looked around. The room was tiled halfway up with cream-coloured tiles. The walls and ceiling were painted white. The floor was alternately covered with white and black tiles.

On the tiled window ledge lay a shaving brush and soap, as well as a razor that Elisabeth had already provided for Franz's homecoming. Now he would use these things instead of Franz.

Sadly, he creamed his face with the soap and carefully removed his reddish-blond fuzz from his cheeks and chin with the sharp razor.

Just as he finished, Elisabeth came in with a large pot of hot, steaming water, which she poured into the tin bathtub.

Aiden was embarrassed to have to be served by Elizabeth, but when he offered to help, she declined with a shake of her head and soon returned again with a steaming pot of water.

Now three more pots of cold water followed. She added a small bar of soap and then asked him to undress and put his clothes outside the bathroom door.

She left the room and left Aiden to himself.

Elisabeth leaned against the living room door and took a deep breath.

She was running away from the truth. The truth that Aiden would tell her about Franz's death. Everything in her resisted wanting to hear this truth, even though it was important to her to know how her beloved Franz had spent his last hours before he died.

It was so hard for her to accept this. Tears stood in her eyes and she felt a deep pain in her chest that she could hardly stand.

As long as she distracted herself, it seemed bearable, but as soon as she allowed the thought of Franz and his death, the pain threatened to break her into a thousand pieces.

How much they had loved each other. They trusted each other and shared everything.

And now she was alone, certain that he would never return home.

She heard the boy put his clothes in front of the bathroom door.

Quickly, taking a deep breath, she lifted her shoulders, rubbed the tears from her face and picked up the clothes and took them to the small kitchen.

There was a washing tub in the corner. Again she heated water, put the laundry in the tub, sprinkled some powder on it and poured the hot water and some cold water on it.

Then she brewed a pot of coffee.

Only a few days ago she had received some coffee powder as a gift from a neighbour and had saved the powder for Franz's return home.

Now she would drink the coffee with the boy while listening to his story.

Aiden, meanwhile, sat in the tin bathtub and enjoyed the warm water. He felt like he was in paradise and thought gratefully of Elisabeth and also of Franz.

It seemed she had not called the police to come and get him. Aiden now knew he could trust her and hoped she would help him remain undetected until there was a way he could return home.

He looked appraisingly at his injured leg, which had healed well but looked very scarred and crippled. He had to accept that it would not get any better. But he knew that was the least of the evils he had to endure. He had been very lucky so far and he was becoming more and more aware of that.

When he had soaped himself thoroughly and washed his reddish-blond hair, which was now a little longer again, he got out of the tin tub and dried himself with the towel Elisabeth had laid out and brushed his still damp hair straight.

He carefully slipped into Franz's long grey pants and slowly pulled them over his injured leg. He slipped on the striped flannel shirt and finally the dark brown trousers, which were much too long for him and also much too wide at the waist. But straps made of grey rubber were attached to the trousers. He slipped the straps over his shoulder and looked down at himself. Finally, he rolled up the trouser legs.

Aiden stepped out of the bathroom and opened the living room door that was ajar.

The coffee cups were already ready on the dining table, along with some bread and honey.

He sat down as Elisabeth was still fiddling around in the kitchen.

As she sat down at the dining table with the coffee pot in her hand, Aiden saw that her eyes were red from crying.

Ashamed, he lowered his gaze. He enjoyed her caring and almost forgot why he was allowed to be here at all.

Elisabeth poured the black, spicy-smelling coffee into his cup and pushed milk and sugar across the table.

Aiden only knew coffee from the front kitchen, but it was made of malt and tasted very thin, almost like water. You could only guess at the taste of coffee. And at home in Ireland there was only tea.

Suspiciously, he took a hearty gulp before finally adding some milk and then taking another sip with relish.

"Do you like it?" asked Elisabeth.

"Yes, very good. Thank you."

Elisabeth looked at him expectantly. Aiden did not know how to begin.

It was not easy for him to talk about the time at the front and his encounter with Franz there in the bomb crater. But he had to explain to her what Franz had done for him.

"Where did you meet Franz?",

Aiden leaned back, keeping his gaze lowered to his fingers, which were resting in his lap and rubbing together nervously. Then he lifted his gaze and began to narrate.

First he talked very fast and Elisabeth raised her hand and stopped his flow of words because she didn't understand everything.

"Please speak more slowly Aiden. I can't understand everything otherwise."

Aiden nodded.

A little quieter, he slowly began to tell his story.

He started when the British soldiers had visited him at home and in his naivety he had followed them to go to war with them.

162

Then his first missions in France at the front, where all the untrained soldiers were sent forward to the battlefield as cannon fodder.

Aiden told her about his fear and the many dead soldiers. All of the cruelty, some of which he couldn't even find the words to express what he had experienced in the relatively short time he spent there. Then he came to the day of the great battle at the Sommè.

He falteringly told her that this day was his 19th birthday, when this great battle was finally opened. He still could not remember everything.

He only knew that on that day he ran like mad onto the vast battlefield and at that moment nothing mattered to him. Whether he would die or survive no longer mattered to him, because even surviving there was cruel.

And then he got to the point in his narrative when he fell into this bomb crater with Franz.

Here his narration faltered and he took another sip of coffee. Elisabeth looked at him the whole time with horror and compassion as she listened tensely to his story.

We kept hearing all kinds of stories about how bad it really was at the front.

Films were shown in some cinemas. But these films glorified the action on the front lines and only showed images of proud soldiers holding up their hands in a fist to fight. After all, they were only propaganda films that did not show the population the cruelty and the real reality.

"And that's where you met Franz?"

"Yes. I was thrown away by the pressure directly when a cannonball hit and fell into a bomb crater from an earlier bomb and landed directly on Franz, who had already been lying in it badly wounded. «

Elisabeth looked at him in horror.

"What injuries did he have?" she asked quietly, deep sorrow etched on her face. "Please tell me."

Aiden continued and described to her about Franz's severe stomach injury. Then how he was startled when Franz looked at him, face to face, and realised he was an enemy and from the German side.

That he, Aiden, had run too far to the German front line. That to this day he didn't know how he had managed this long distance to get there. He must have been out of his mind and lost all sense of time and pain.

Aiden told Elisabeth that Franz, like him, was frozen with fear at first. But then Franz spoke to him, in English, and asked him what his name was and where he came from.

After a while, Franz told him his plan, that he, Aiden, should return in his place, with his name, to Munich, to his wife.

Elisabeth listened to him attentively.

"Believe me, Elisabeth, I didn't want this and I rejected this plan at first," Aiden exclaimed in exasperation. "I said to him that help would come soon. But Franz said that he knew he would not survive. He felt his injury was too severe."

Aiden slapped his hands in front of his face and then wearily ran his hand through his now already dried hair. Elisabeth stood up and walked around the table to the boy and put her hand comfortingly on his shoulder.

"It's all right, my boy. It's not your fault. You're just another victim of this dreadful war. And I believe you didn't kill him."

Aiden looked up at her gratefully.

"What happened to your leg?", Elisabeth then wanted to know.

Aiden showed Elisabeth his leg injury, who could imagine from the scars and mutilations how badly the leg had been hurt.

She stroked his head comfortingly.

Then she wanted to know what happened next.

"What did Franz say? Tell me exactly. Please," Elisabeth looked at him imploringly and sat back down in her chair.

Aiden repeated, as best as his memory would allow, everything Franz had said to him.

He told her about Franz's words about their happy marriage and that he had promised Franz to deliver the letter to her if the plan succeeded.

Elisabeth listened to him intently so that she understood everything he said.

Sometimes she would raise her hand and ask him to repeat what he had said.

All the while, she held her handkerchief in front of her mouth, from which painful sounds kept coming out, which she tried to suppress.

"Please believe me Elisabeth. I tried to talk him out of it when he suggested we swap roles and uniforms. I didn't want him to die. He became almost like a brother to me in that short time we spoke, when we should have been enemies. But he insisted on this role reversal and we had little time. Franz was getting weaker by the minute," he spoke in a softer voice. "I finally agreed, in my fear. And we changed uniforms as best we could."

"And then?" whispered Elisabeth tonelessly.

"Before we were even finished, he died in my arms," Aiden replied, his voice choked with tears.

Elisabeth stood up frantically and stepped to the window, leaning on the sill. Tears ran down her cheeks and her shoulders shook.

Aiden stood up as well. Somewhat awkwardly, he stepped up to Elisabeth at the window and put a hand on her trembling shoulder.

He did not know what to say. There were no words of comfort. Especially not from him, as he was aware.

After a while, Elizabeth turned and looked at Aiden, who was still standing next to her with his hand on her shoulder.

"I will help you as best I can.

That is the only thing I can still do for Franz. I will fulfil his wish to help you," she whispered in a tear-stained voice, but could no longer hold back her tears.

Tears were now running down Aiden's cheeks too.

"Thank you!" he whispered. "Thank you for believing me. I was very afraid you would think I was a fraud. I would have understood. But I can assure you, everything I told you is the truth."

"Don't worry about it. I believe you. Because just as you told it, my Franz would act. He had a big heart even in his last hour."

They stood at the window for a while and talked about the cruelty of the war, which no one could escape. To which they were exposed with all the helplessness and pain.

Later they sat down at the table again and Aiden ate his honey bread. Elisabeth pushed her plate away. She could not bring herself to eat a bite.

"I still have a small room here where there is all kinds of old junk and also an old bed. You can help me clear out the room in the next few days. Until then, you can sleep here on the sofa."

"Thank you Elisabeth," Aiden whispered softly.

"Now you go to sleep for a while. You look very exhausted. And so am I. Later we'll sit down again and discuss how we want to proceed. We have to think carefully about how to integrate you here, because you can't stay locked up in the flat unseen forever," she said with a thoughtful expression.

"But for a certain time it won't be any different. At least as long as you don't understand and speak our language."

"Thank you!" Aiden couldn't find any other words to express what he was feeling right now. Relief, helplessness, gratitude, fear.

He was dependent on Elisabeth and her help.

But what could he give back to her? Could he really ask her to protect him? And if she did anyway, he was aware that he had met his guardian angel. First in the form of Franz, who had sent him on this journey, and then in the form of Elisabeth, who wanted to help him. Aiden suddenly stood up and went out of the room to look for his uniform jacket. Elisabeth looked up in amazement.

"What are you doing?" she called after him.

"Just a moment, I'll be right back. I have something to show you."

When he returned to the living room, he held his golden coin in his hand and placed it on the table in front of Elisabeth. The latter looked at the coin and then at him in amazement.

"What is it?" She did not tell him that she had already discovered this coin in his jacket.

"This is a golden coin that I was given as a child by a leprechaun, a goblin."

Elisabeth looked at him sceptically. Perhaps he is not in his right mind, she thought in dismay.

But Aiden continued unperturbed.

"I was eight years old and engrossed in my play outside our cottage, when suddenly he stood in front of me and showed me his coin.

I was looking at coins that had rolled to my feet.

The goblin gave me one of the two coins as a gift. He said to me: 'Always keep it with you and it will bring you luck and save you from any situation, no matter how hopeless. And I took it with me to war and it has always protected me. Now it has led me to you through Franz. And now you want to help me," he looked thoughtfully at the coin.

"I never thought before about the power of this coin and the truth about its influence on my life. I'm not even sure if I might have dreamt it all back then and found the coin by chance and just spun a fantasy story. But now nothing can stop me from believing in it. Yes, to believe in miracles," he concluded his thoughts, which he had spoken aloud.

Elisabeth looked at him compassionately and lovingly, as a mother looks at her son when she senses his distress and would most like to take this heavy burden from him.

She could not believe his story about the goblin, but she understood him and did not contradict him.

Elisabeth could not help but immediately take this boy into her heart.

Any feeling of hatred or that he was to blame for her husband's death was far from her mind.

Not even in her great pain, which raged fresh and cruel within her, could she hate this boy for being an enemy who had shot the men of her country.

He was a boy who did not know what he was getting into. when he went off to war.

A boy who was far removed from any desire to fight or euphoria for war, and at home, a heartbroken mother is surely waiting for news of her boy.

She may have already received the news that her son had been killed, after they had found her Franz and assigned him to the British and found out his identity from his identification tag, which came from Aiden, and then told the family. What a drama for everyone. It brought tears to Elisabeth's eyes again.

She put her hand on Aidens, in which he held the golden coin.

"It is a beautiful thought that this coin has such magical powers. What is more precious than to really believe in something. If the belief is strong enough, then this belief will also show itself in reality. I am convinced of that."

Aiden looked at Elizabeth gratefully, for not thinking he was crazy.

"That's exactly what my mother used to say to me."

Elisabeth withdrew her hand and leaned back in her chair thoughtfully.

"Did I perhaps not believe strongly enough that Franz would come back healthy from the war?" she whispered, more to herself than to Aiden.

Suddenly she shook her head.

"No, I didn't believe in it strongly enough. I wanted to believe it, but I had doubts about it every day. I could not believe it deep inside me.

I was afraid of bad news every day."

Aiden looked at Elizabeth, startled.

"But it's not your fault that Franz died. It's war and it can happen to anyone, at any time and anywhere at the front," he cried agitatedly.

Elisabeth looked up sadly.

"You're probably right. Then maybe I anticipated that he wouldn't come home and that's why I couldn't believe it," she mused to herself.

Elisabeth felt an incredible despair within herself and searched with all her might for a cause, for a

misconduct on her part as to why this fate had befallen her and Franz.

Aiden looked at the golden coin in his hand.

"Do you think the coin will take me back? Back to Ireland to my family?" he looked up from the coin hopefully.

Elisabeth looked at him thoughtfully.

"Yes, I believe in it. I can feel it coming true. You will see your family again." she finally replied with conviction and smiled at Aiden.

At her words, a smile also crossed Aiden's face.

For a while neither of them spoke a word and each was lost in their own thoughts. Suddenly Elisabeth stood up, pulled her shoulders up and took a few deep breaths.

"I'm going to do some quick shopping for the next few days. We'll have a lot to do and you won't be out in public for a while. «

She took the dishes from the table and brought everything into the kitchen.

"My friend Greta, whom you have already met, lives one floor above me and I have to let her know that you are staying with me for a while.

I don't want her to get suspicious and think that I'm hiding you here in the flat. I tell her that you are a distant relative of Franz, traumatised and unable to hear or speak. And that I will help you when you are healthy again, since your parents are no longer alive. Then hopefully we'll have peace from her prying questions and glances."

Aiden looked at her gratefully before he got up and lay down exhausted on the sofa with the golden coin in his hand. He saw Elisabeth go into the bathroom to freshen her face and remove the tear stains and leave the flat. Shortly afterwards, he had already fallen asleep.

*

When Elisabeth returned to the flat, Aiden was still fast asleep. It was almost eight o'clock in the evening by now. Elisabeth had gone up to her friend Greta's after shopping to tell her about Aiden.

As she stood in front of Greta's door, it suddenly occurred to her that they hadn't even talked about Aiden's new name yet. He needs another first name. In seconds, dozens of first names rushed through her head.

But what would Aiden like? Could she just pick a name without him?

But now when she tells Greta that the boy is staying with her, she has to tell her his name.

171

Elisabeth was getting all hot. She had already rung Greta's doorbell, otherwise she would go downstairs again and talk to Aiden first.

But now it was too late. The door was opened from the inside and Greta received her with a compassionate, sad face. "My dear Elisabeth, how are you? Come in. I wanted to go downstairs and look in on you. But no one answered when I rang the bell."

"Thank you Greta. That's sweet of you. I went out for some air and did some shopping. It did me good."

"Come in.", Greta asked her and stepped aside.

"Yes just for a moment. I have to go back downstairs in a minute. I have a visitor," Elisabeth told her.

Greta turned indignantly to Elisabeth.

"You really let this young, ragged soldier into your flat? Elisabeth I am horrified. What does he want from you?"

"He is a distant relative of Franz. A cousin on his father's side sent him here because his parents have been dead for a long time and she couldn't take him in," Elisabeth answered quickly, surprised at herself that this lie came so easily to her lips. "I didn't know him before either," she continued quickly, before Greta could interject. "But he wrote everything down for me, because he is totally traumatised by a grenade hit and can't hear or speak.

And he gave me a letter from his aunt, who sent him here, asking if I could look after him as long as he didn't have to go back to the front. This aunt didn't know that I would get the news of Franz's death just today."

Overcome by sudden grief, tears came to her eyes and Greta went to her and took her in her arms.

Suddenly Greta raised her head.

"But the boy brought you the letter from Franz. You told me that yourself," she looked at Elisabeth suspiciously.

Elisabeth felt a chill run down her spine.

She had no longer thought about the fact that Greta already knew that the boy had brought her the letter from Franz. She had told her herself. Her thoughts searched frantically for a credible answer.

To buy herself time, she started crying again, which was not difficult for her, before she finally had the saving idea.

"The letter was lying outside my flat door, the boy told me. He had just lifted it up when I came up the stairs. And then he held it out to me, so that at first I thought he had brought the letter with him. He couldn't tell me because he couldn't speak. It wasn't until just now that he wrote it all down for me," Elisabeth explained to her through her tears.

"It's all right, my dear. I'm here if you need me. But please be careful with the young man. You never know. Even if he is a relative, you can never fathom his intentions," Greta replied, however, with great suspicion in her voice.

"What is his name?" she asked suddenly.

Beads of sweat formed on Elisabeth's forehead with excitement. In a split second she thought.

"Fritz. Fritz is his name." she finally called out. "Fritz von Letten." she quickly completed the name.

In the short time available, she had thought of choosing a short, one-syllable name so that Aiden would find it easier to pronounce.

Greta only nodded when she heard the name, but still looked at Elisabeth with suspicion in her eyes.

They talked for a while longer, then Elisabeth said goodbye and left her friend's flat relieved.

She really liked Greta, but she often thought that Greta was very hard on other people, trusted only a few people and did not let anyone get close to her easily who could or was allowed to conquer her heart. She lacked a loving heart. But at heart she was a good soul. Elisabeth had never found out what had made Greta so hard. Although they confided a great deal in each other, Greta kept this locked deep inside. And since Elisabeth had a good heart by nature, she could also accept this and took Greta as she was.

*

The following day Elisabeth and Aiden spent clearing out and cleaning the small room so that he could sleep in his own room.
When they had finished, there was only a bed, a chest of drawers and a chair left in the room.
Elisabeth washed the curtains and drapes and cleaned the floor, which had not been cleaned for a long time.
Throughout the day, she held objects out to Aiden and explained the German words for them.
Aiden tried as best he could to remember the words. Some were not difficult at all, others he lost right away.
In the hallway there was now a hodgepodge of things, such as a broken chair, two rather battered woven laundry baskets, two old picture frames covered with mould stains and an old suitcase with used clothes of Elisabeth's that she had not worn for a long time.
After this exhausting day, Aiden felt very exhausted and tired.

He realised that it would take some time before he regained his strength. However, Elisabeth did everything she could to bring him up and give him enough food.

In the evening of that day, she sat over the propaganda sheets and newspapers to catch up on the events of the war, which was mercilessly running its course.

From Aiden's stories, Elisabeth now knew that the news that reached her here in Munich did not correspond to what was really happening there in France.

The situation became more and more threatening for everyone. The food emergency was getting bigger and bigger and there were so many men spread out on the fronts that many women were now also called upon to do the men's work.

Elisabeth had long been considering signing up as a conductor at the tram depot, as there was a great shortage there and this job paid well, better than her work at the military hospital.

Aiden couldn't send her off to look for work, she had to keep him hidden or they would send him straight back to the front.

His leg had healed well and he could already walk effortlessly without crutches.

She was aware that Aiden would have to stay in the flat for a long time before he could be seen outside among other people. So he would not be able to contribute anything to her livelihood.

They had to think about that, because their savings would not last forever. And the little she earned as an auxiliary nurse in the military hospital was just enough for herself.

Elisabeth had decided to return to the hospital in two days so that the pay would not be too long. All the work and distraction with Aiden did her good and it was only in the evening, when peace returned and Aiden had retired to his room, that the sadness and pain flooded her again and she let her tears run free.

*

So the next few days passed very quickly. She spent six hours a day in the hospital, hurried home and taught Aiden the remaining hours, gradually teaching him the German language. Aiden found it surprisingly easy to remember the vocabulary and grammar.

She made him a notebook and gave him many tasks for each day to learn by the evening.

On two evenings the doorbell rang and Greta stood at the flat door wanting to talk to her. Elisabeth was reluctant to let her into the flat.

She didn't want her to come into contact with Aiden.

That is why she told her every time that she would like to be alone to process her grief.

Elisabeth evaded Greta as best she could and explained that the boy was still with her, but there was still no improvement with his hearing and speech. That he was still very exhausted and slept a lot.

Greta listened to her suspiciously, but finally accepted Elisabeth's wish to be alone. However, she asked her to call if she needed someone to talk to. Elisabeth reassured her that she would definitely get in touch.

For Greta, however, it was very suspicious that her friend was withdrawing from her so much. And her suspicion that it also had something to do with this boy increased day by day.

In those first weeks, Aiden did not go outside. Too much fear that he would be exposed by some circumstance prevented him from doing so.

Although he quickly learned the new language, it was still clearly audible through the accent that it was not his mother tongue.

Elisabeth knew that this would be the most difficult task for Aiden, to eradicate and discard this accent.

Every day she did speech exercises with him and noticed that it was almost easier to teach him the language in Munich dialect than in High German. This made it easier to suppress the accent.

Sometimes he pronounced sentences so well that she could no longer tell the difference. But there was still a lot for him to learn.

At the same time, she taught him to write German so that he could at least write his name and address. Everything else would follow.

It would still be a long road.

Aiden was still behaving very eagerly and calmly, but Elisabeth was worried about how he would cope in the long run with being locked up in the flat most of the time.

Munich
December 1916

Six weeks later, Elisabeth and Aiden were sitting at the dining table in the evening, leafing through the latest news edition about the war.

Elisabeth read aloud:

"Today, December 12, 1916, a peace offer was made by the Central Powers. At the insistence of Austria-Hungary, this peace note was pronounced after the conquest of Romania. "

Elisabeth jumped up and was about to burst into jubilation, as she hoped so much that this war would soon come to an end. But then she sat down again and continued reading:

"Whether this peace offer will be accepted by the hostile governments cannot be foreseen and will require a while of waiting and hoping. "

All the while, Aiden watched Elisabeth and didn't quite understand why she had suddenly jumped up so enthusiastically.

He was still struggling to understand the context of her words.

Elisabeth calmed down again and sat down next to Aiden and slowly explained to him once more what she had just read out and what it would mean for him once the war was over.

Namely, that he could soon travel back to his home country. Of course, only when everything had calmed down. But it would be foreseeable once the war was over.

Aiden listened intently and then understood what she was trying to tell him and a happy grin crossed his face and reached his eyes, which began to sparkle at the thought of soon seeing his beloved Ireland and family again.

Aiden stood up and fell around Elisabeth's neck, lifting her up with joy.

"Stop, Aiden, put me down. It's not time yet. We have to wait and see if the peace offer is accepted," she tried to dampen his exuberant joy.

"Oh come on, it's going to come true. I have every faith in it," Aiden rejoiced and never stopped grinning.

Then he told Elisabeth for the hundredth time about Ireland and the lush green meadows, about the legends and sagas, the fairies and goblins and about his family.

He wanted her to travel with him to Ireland so that he could introduce her to his family and wanted to show her his country and thus thank her for all that she was doing for him. Elisabeth had her hands full trying to reassure Aiden. If she had known how much he was hoping, she would have been more careful with what she told him. But she had been so pleased herself about this announcement that she had not thought about it.

*

The days passed. Elisabeth went to the military hospital for a few hours in the morning and at home she taught Aiden. She still cried herself to sleep every night and mourned Franz.

She often thought that life just went on as if nothing had happened. Everything and everyone around her continued to live as before, only for her everything had changed.

At many moments it was very difficult for her to accept this. But she saw on the streets, the many war wounded and many a war widow like herself and knew that she was not alone with this fate. Strangely enough, that gave her some comfort. In the end she was grateful that Franz had sent Aiden to her. She was not alone because of his presence. With Aiden, she had a task she could devote herself to and which distracted her. And her great goal was that Aiden could one day return to his homeland.

*

Soon Christmas was just around the corner.

Greta rang the doorbell two days before Christmas and brought Elisabeth a small, waist-high, very skinny Christmas tree.

Elisabeth opened the door just a tiny crack and looked first at the tree and then at Greta in amazement. She quickly realised that Greta intended to be invited by her to the Christmas feast.

In the last few weeks they had rarely seen each other and when they did, Elisabeth went to see her, one floor up, in the flat.

Greta was still very suspicious about the young man in Elisabeth's flat. But she no longer said a word to Elisabeth about the young man, but she always had more than one eye on what was going on. As far as she could observe, young Fritz did not leave the flat.

Only once had she seen from her window how they had left the house in the evening and returned an hour later.

But as soon as she asked Elisabeth about the boy, she evaded her and quickly steered the conversation to another topic. She couldn't get anything out of her.

So now she was standing in front of Elisabeth's door with the Christmas tree.

"Greta, did you get yourself a Christmas tree?"

"This is for you," Greta replied, holding the tree out to her. "Or do you already have one?"

"No, I haven't got one yet. Thank you for thinking of me."

Elisabeth now opened the door fully, but remained undecided, standing in the middle of the doorframe, for she did not know whether she should invite Greta in.

Greta looked at her questioningly and waited for the prompt. Elisabeth felt backed into a corner and found no credible excuse.

Finally, she had no choice if she didn't want to be rude and invited her in, hoping that Aiden had followed the conversation and retired to his room.

Greta entered the hallway and put the Christmas tree down on the floor before opening her coat and taking it off.

"Is the boy here too? What was his name again? Fritz said you, right?", Greta asked in a seemingly uninterested tone, while she hung her coat on the coat rack hook.

"Yes, Fritz is here. But I think he already retired to his room when I was in the kitchen earlier."

Elisabeth hoped that Aiden had taken the hint. Then she asked Greta into the living room, which she found empty. Elisabeth was relieved.

"How is he doing? Can he speak and hear again?", Greta asked curiously.

"The hearing is already almost completely back. He understands when I say something to him. But he is not making any progress with his speech yet," Elisabeth lied without making a face.

Her heart began to pound and she was afraid Greta would hear the tremor in her voice.

Greta, however, showed no movement and looked around. She looked curiously into the kitchen to see if she could spot the boy in there. But he was not to be seen there either.

"As I said, he is safe in his room. He reads a lot," Elisabeth said with relief. "Would you like some tea Greta?"

"Yes with pleasure. «

Elisabeth went into the kitchen and took a deep breath while she put the tea water on.

After a few minutes she returned with the teapot and two cups on a tray and they sat down at the dining table.

"Have you already been told where Franz fell and when exactly?" asked Greta curiously.

Elisabeth had to work hard at the lump to swallow that formed in her throat, she found it hard at Greta's question before she could answer.

"Yes," she answered hesitantly. "I got some mail."

Greta looked at her in amazement.

"You haven't told me about that yet?"

"The letter came only a few days ago," Elisabeth replied quickly.

Greta looked at her suspiciously again.

"So, where did he fall?"

"It was on 6 September at the Sommé in West Flanders. He fell at the very beginning of the battle. More soldiers fell on that first day of this battle, which went on for weeks, than ever before in one day. That's why it took so long for the news of his death to come."

Tears came to Elisabeth's eyes and she put her hands in front of her face.

And although she knew she had just lied, since there was no letter, she knew from Aiden that she was speaking the truth. And she knew that her Franz was now in some mass grave in France with many more dead. And that he was buried there as an Irish soldier because he was wearing Aiden's uniform.

Greta jumped up from her chair and ran around the table to Elisabeth and put her arm around her shoulder comfortingly.

"Thank you Greta. I'm fine," taking a deep breath, Elisabeth straightened up in her chair and took Greta's hand, which was resting on her shoulder.

"Glad you're here. I'm sorry I've had so little time for you in the last few weeks. But I need a lot of time for myself at the moment and I have to take care of the boy and take care of me too."

"I am worried about you, Elisabeth. This blow of fate that you have to cope with and then also the strange boy in your flat. Are you sure everything is all right?" Greta did not let go of her concerns.

"Yes really Greta, it's all right. Come sit back down and have a cup of tea with me."

Elisabeth grabbed the teapot and poured for Greta.

"You know, the boy is good for me. He can answer my questions about the front and the fighting there. He brings me so close to Franz when he writes everything down, even if they are cruel stories. And he needs my help, now that he has no other relatives to look after him until he is completely well again. It does me good not to be alone here in the flat."

Greta sipped her tea thoughtfully.

"And how long are you going to give him shelter here in your flat?"

"As long as he needs my help, and as long as I can prevent him from having to go back to the front as best I can, I will house him here and also hide him if I have to," Elisabeth replied resolutely, looking at Greta militantly.

Elisabeth knew that Greta was very suspicious of the boy. She would watch her and the boy like a Lux, at every turn.

Therefore, she now had to be a little more offensive for Greta to be her ally without telling her the true background of Aiden's origin and avoid his betrayal.

Something was holding her back from revealing the whole truth to Greta. Elisabeth was afraid that she would betray Aiden? It was just such an inner feeling that it was better to just keep this secret to herself.

Greta looked at her in horror.

"You want to keep him hidden here with you? Then he's a deserter?"

"Yes, if I have to, I will keep him hidden until the war is over."

Challengingly, Elisabeth looked Greta in the eye before she continued. "So far he couldn't be sent back to the front for health reasons, but his hearing has already improved and if he is discovered on the road by the patrols, they will surely take him away, despite his lost speech. I want to prevent that at all costs."

"But you can't put yourself in danger like that for this strange boy."

Upset, Greta jumped up from her chair again. "You'll be locked up if they catch you. If anyone finds out you're hiding a strong young man here who should be fighting for his fatherland."

Elisabeth also jumped up from her chair and went to the window and looked down at the street through the curtains. "No one will discover us. We'll be careful," she finally said firmly.

"Unless you betray me? " Elisabeth turned to Greta and looked at her provocatively.

"I will not betray you. You're my friend. " Greta rowed back indignantly and approached Elisabeth. "Do you really think I'm capable of that?" Greta looked at Elisabeth in horror.

"No, Greta, I'm sorry. But it's very difficult for me."

"Elisabeth, you can trust me. I will not betray you. My word of honour on that. But I ask that you be very careful and take care of yourself. Will you promise me that?"

Elisabeth nodded in agreement and inwardly breathed a sigh of relief.

This hurdle had been cleared for the time being, she thought with relief.

"So, but now you tell me exactly how you want to manage it all. Will he stay in the flat the whole time, and how long will he be able to keep it up?" Greta looked at her curiously.

"He is a very sweet and patient boy. Now I want to make sure that he is completely healthy. You should see his injured leg. How terribly he must have been hurt. It still causes him problems. And I want to do everything I can to help him find his speech again. It will take time to heal these inner wounds. And I think that until then it won't be a problem for him to stay here in this sheltered flat. Every now and then, in the evening, when it's already dusk, I walk him around the block a few times to give him some fresh air.

But going further into town or spending longer time outside would be too dangerous for him."

"Yes, I understand. But will you be able to provide his daily food in the long run? Is your money enough for that?"

"That worries me a little too. ", Elisabeth admitted. "But I was thinking of applying for a job as a conductor at the tram depot. They earn good money and it's not such strenuous work."

Greta looked at her in surprise.

"You want to stop working at the military hospital?"

"Yes, if I get the job as a conductor, I will stop there. I would earn almost double at the depot," Elisabeth replied.

Greta seemed to be thinking.

"Actually, you are right. Women are wanted there as conductors because all the men are at the front. Not such a bad idea, actually," Greta mused further. "Maybe I'll apply there with you. A bit more money couldn't hurt. And to be honest, I can't stand the drone of a military hospital head nurse any more."

Greta looked at Elisabeth with a laugh and held out her hand to decide on their project, which Greta had now appointed as their joint project.

"And I assure you of my full support with the boy. Whenever you need help, you let me know. Do you promise me?"

"But I have to promise you a lot today," Elisabeth laughed, but then gratefully accepted Greta's hand and embraced it warmly.

"So now you just have to invite me to Christmas. After all, I brought you a Christmas tree." Greta looked mischievously at Elisabeth and shrugged her shoulders innocently.

Elisabeth had to laugh out loud as she looked into Greta's unfimiliar mischievous face.

"Of course you are welcome to come on Christmas Eve. Now we just have to find meat for the Christmas roast somewhere."

"I think I have an idea. I'll let you know tomorrow. You take care of everything else, I'll bring the roast."

They both talked for a while about their application to the tram depot and immediately decided to present themselves there tomorrow, after duty at the military hospital.

When Greta had left the flat, Aiden cautiously crept out of his room.

"Is she gone?"

"Yes, don't worry. She has already left. I told her that you will stay with me longer and that I want to keep you hidden though, so that they don't send you back to the front."

Aiden looked at her anxiously. "And how did she react?"

"She is very worried about me, but she has accepted it and will not tell on us. By the way, she will celebrate Christmas with us. Better said, Christmas Eve."

Aiden looked at her in amazement and sat down on the sofa. "Christmas Eve? How do you celebrate Christmas here in Germany? We always had roast lamb on Christmas Eve. And the next morning we were allowed to unwrap a present."

Lost in memories, Aiden looked down at his hands.

"How will my parents and sister spend Christmas this year?"

Elisabeth looked at him sympathetically and sat down next to him and put an arm reassuringly around his slender shoulders.

"You will certainly be very sad. But I'm sure your parents will feel that you're still alive and won't give up hope."

"Oh if only I could write them a letter or send them some kind of sign."

Aiden leaned into Elizabeth's protective arm.

"Think very hard of them and send them your love and your thoughts and they will feel it."

She had already grown very fond of this boy and didn't even want to imagine what his parents must be going through right now because of all the worry about him.

"Come, help me peel the potatoes and prepare dinner. And you tell me at work how you spent your Christmas. »

Elisabeth wanted to pull him out of his cloudy thoughts, got up and pulled Aiden up from the sofa, who immediately followed her into the kitchen.

He was always happy when he had something practical to do and could help Elisabeth.

He used the many hours he spent alone in the flat to complete the study workload that Elisabeth gave him every day.

And while he walked around the flat, he practised aloud the pronunciation of the German words he had newly learned.

Day by day it got better, but his Irish accent was still audible. He knew he still had a long way to go.

Elisabeth always said to him that they would manage to get him to speak German perfectly by the time the war finally ended.

*

And so the year 1916 drew to a close. Elisabeth and Aiden had spent Christmas with Greta. Greta had managed to get hold of a large piece of roast beef. Where she got it, she kept to herself with a smile.

Elisabeth prepared a wonderful roast from it, which she arranged on the plates with some beans and potatoes. To celebrate Christmas Day we had a cake with preserved plums for dessert.

On the small Christmas tree, white wax candles burned between lushly applied tinsel, which spread radiant light through the candlelight.

Greta bought them a bottle of red wine, which they drank from the old, heavy crystal goblets that Elisabeth had been given by her godmother for her wedding to Franz.

The table was festively set and in the middle was a small pot with a Christmas rose that Elisabeth had discovered at the market when she was buying potatoes and beans. Three beautiful white flowers adorned the deep green of the leaves and she could not resist buying them.

The gramophone that Elisabeth had received from Franz three years ago for Christmas was playing the Christmas carol "Silent Night, Holy Night".

When she had already put the record on once in the afternoon as she was decorating the Christmas tree, tears ran down her face at the memory of the wonderful Christmas she was able to spend with Franz.

Then, a few months later, the war began and in the following years she always spent Christmas alone, without her beloved Franz, who was serving at the front. Only once was he here at her home on home leave, for three weeks.

That was in the summer of 1915.

Despite the immense joy at being reunited, the three weeks were overshadowed and very difficult for Elisabeth. Franz was physically unharmed, but the psychological wounds Franz had brought home with him had changed him greatly. He did not speak a word about what he had experienced there at the front and would have to experience again when he returned. Instead, he covered up and repressed the thoughts of it as best he could. But often he stared into space, lost in thought, and had tears in his eyes.

Elisabeth did not ask any more questions when she realised that he did not want to talk about it.

They sat together on the sofa for hours. Nestled close together, she cradled him in her arms and many a time tears ran wordlessly down his face.

She accepted it quietly and wanted nothing more than to be able to help him.

The farewell after the three weeks was quiet.

Elisabeth felt how much Franz was fighting inside to stay strong and not show his fear.

Then he had quickly boarded the train.

She waved after him for a long time before settling down on a wooden bench at the station and surrendering to her pain. That was the last time they had seen each other. But a letter from Franz came regularly, at intervals of a month.

He had always liked to write and Elisabeth had the feeling that it was easier for him to reveal his feelings in written words than in the spoken word.

And so she was able to look into his soul, at least to a small extent, in the letters.

Even if he spared her cruel details, he revealed his fears, but also his hopes, to her through what he wrote.

She loved reading his letters.

She had an old, beautiful tin box in her bedroom where she kept the letters and often read them again and again when she was lying in bed. She felt very close to him and hoped that maybe he could feel that where he was.

Even now after his death, she often read these letters and heard his voice in his words.

*

She was still standing by the gramophone, deep in her memories, when Aiden joined her.

"Elisabeth, what is that beautiful song?"

Aiden's words snapped her out of her thoughts and she turned to him in surprise.

"You don't know this song? It's called 'Silent Night, Holy Night' Don't you know it in Ireland?"

"I have never heard it before. I can't remember.

We didn't have one of those gramotones or whatever this is called at home."

"A gramophone," Elisabeth corrected him with a smile.

Aiden listened for a while.

"Such a beautiful song. But it makes me a little sad."

"Yes, you're right. ", Elisabeth replied. "Music goes deep into our heart and opens it wide, so that the sadness and pain you have buried deep inside can flow freely to the surface. It would be different if you were very happy right now, then this music, these sounds, would make you even happier because it opens your heart wide and your feelings of happiness and emotion that are inside you right now can flow to the surface."

Aiden listened to Elisabeth with fascination and felt deeply inside himself. Yes, the music reached him very deeply. Then he heard Elisabeth continue to speak.

"Often, when I sat with Franz in front of the gramophone and listened to the music, he would tell me to listen to myself. To pay attention to what emotions the music was awakening in me. Music is capable of so much. It brings out what is moving you inside. It can make you laugh or cry."

Sadly, she turned back to the gramophone and took the tone arm off the record when the song was over.

"But now I have to put the roast in the oven so that it will be ready on time at six o'clock when Greta arrives." With these words she tried to push away her sadness.

"Can I listen to the song again?" asked Aiden.

"Later, when we are sitting at dinner. You still have to do your language exercises so that you don't make a mistake tonight," she reminded him admonishingly.

"I really have to get into the habit of calling you Fritz. I always forget when we're alone. Fritz, I'll only call you Fritz now, otherwise I'll let the cat out of the bag when Greta is here. "Elisabeth looked at him worriedly.

"Don't worry Elisabeth, if it really slips out, I just won't react to it. We'll work it out. But if you want, I'll just be Fritz now. Even if it's hard for me."

"But it is necessary if we are to make you one of us until the war is over. «

Aiden nodded in agreement, albeit with a sad expression, and went to his room to do his speech exercises.

He looked forward to the evening, to the food and especially to this beautiful music that he could then listen to again. The mood of this music brought him back to his family with his heart and he could feel it.

*

Shortly before six, the doorbell rang.

Elisabeth sent Aiden to the door. He was to greet Greta and lead her into the living room. His first big test in front of an audience, and in front of such a critical and suspicious person as Greta.

Elisabeth had warned Greta that he had probably lost his entire language and was now only gradually finding the words again, but could hardly form complete sentences.

Greta believed her story without asking her any more questions, but Elisabeth still felt her suspicion.

When Aiden opened the door, Greta rushed in singing, with a bottle of red wine in her hand. As she warbled "Oh Tannenbaun, oh Tannenbaum", she looked happily at Aiden.

"Merry Christmas Fritz. Is Elisabeth still in the kitchen? " and had already disappeared into the living room.

Aiden followed her, grinning and nodding.

Greta is a funny woman, he thought. She always seemed so stern, but she could probably also be hilarious and had a demeanour that now made him laugh. What he didn't know was that she was already a little drunk.

When he came into the living room, she opened the red wine and Elisabeth was just bringing the food from the kitchen.

"Fritz, will you please light the candles on the Christmas tree."

She put the plate with the roast on the table, then got the potatoes and vegetables before she went to the gramophone and put the needle on the plate.

After all the candles were lit, Aiden sat down in his place between the two women.

The music sounded softly. The light of the candles spread a pleasant atmosphere in the room and despite all that had happened and all the sadness within him, he felt a gratitude within himself that he was allowed to experience this today.

He looked at Elisabeth, who was distributing the meat on her plates.

She paused for a moment when she felt his gaze on her and tears came to her eyes. They both knew that at that very moment they were thinking of the people they loved.

Greta looked from one to the other, but kept quiet because she did not want to destroy this moment. Sometimes she could even be sensitive, but this was very rare.

When the moment was over, Elisabeth continued to distribute the vegetables and potatoes, Greta poured wine into her glasses and Aiden listened to the music.

The meal was a lot of fun. Greta did everything she could to keep the conversation going and not let sadness set in.

Aiden couldn't understand everything she said, but he could follow most of what she said.

Sometimes Greta spoke directly to him and he tried to find the right words. But sometimes he just shrugged his shoulders and remained silent. It was very exhausting for him.

Elisabeth held her breath a few times, afraid that he might say something that would betray him. But everything went well, even though Greta raised her eyebrows a few times in surprise.

After a few sips of wine, however, everyone's tension eased a little and it became a cosy evening.

After dinner, when the table was cleared, Elisabeth went out of the room for a moment and came back with two small packages in her hand. She handed one of them to Aiden and the other to Greta.

"Ohhh, thank you Elisabeth. Wait a moment," Greta called, jumped up and ran into the hallway.

She also came back with parcels in her hand and handed one of them to Elisabeth and a smaller one she put on the table in front of Aiden.

Aiden looked at the two women in amazement and struggled to compose himself.

"Merry Christmas!" shouted Greta cheerfully, reaching for her parcel and tearing open the paper.

A scarf knitted by Elisabeth herself in various shades of brown was revealed.

"Ohh... thank you Elisabeth. The scarf is beautiful and just right for my coat. Thank you so much."

She jumped up and fell around her neck.

"Now open yours," she urged Elisabeth.

The latter took her package and, unlike Greta, opened it very thoughtfully and carefully. She did not want to damage the paper and keep it. Greta rolled her eyes in amusement.

"Come on, it's just paper."

"Who knows if we'll still have wrapping paper next Christmas if the war never ends.

It won't do any harm if I keep it," Elisabeth explains firmly. Greta just shrugged her shoulders.

"If you say so. I don't think that far ahead. Who knows what will happen."

When Elisabeth had carefully removed the paper, a beautiful pair of finest suede gloves emerged.

"My God Greta, such beautiful gloves and so elegant. They must have cost a fortune? And where did you get them?" Elisabeth breathlessly exclaimed in surprise at the expensive gift.

"Don't worry about it, sweetheart. These are from my aunt. I found them when I was cleaning out her closet after she died. You know she always bought expensive things but then often didn't use them for years. So some things came up that were still stored in the cupboard unused. Also these gloves and I thought that would be a nice Christmas present for you."

"Thank you very much Greta. I appreciate that very much. But it really wasn't necessary."

"Papperlapapp..... a gift is a gift," Greta replied firmly.

Touched, Elisabeth stood up and embraced Greta fervently. She joyfully tried them on right away and held out her gloved hands with elegant movements and turns for their inspection.

All three burst out laughing.

Elisabeth finally asked Aiden to unwrap his presents.

He felt a little uncomfortable because he had a small present for Elisabeth but not for Greta.

Elisabeth handed him the present. He felt the package and knew it had to be a book.

He opened it just as carefully as Elisabeth and then folded the paper carefully. What emerged was indeed a book.

'The Happy Prince and Other Tales' by Oscar Wilde.

"Thank you Elisabeth. I am so pleased to receive the book."

He eagerly leafed through the book with the fairytale-like Stories by Oscar Wilde, his compatriot.

The book was, of course, in German script and it would be a great challenge for him to read it. But he had a lot of time and it would help him a lot to develop his German skills more and more.

"Here, open my present too," Greta called out and pushed the package towards him.

Aiden took it and turned it a few times in his hands. He was really curious to see what Greta would give him. He didn't expect to get anything from her after she had been so suspicious of him.

He removed the paper and was astonished to see a silver-coloured pocket watch in his hands. Immediatel Memories came back to him.

His father also had a similar pocket watch, which he in turn had inherited from his father. And his father always told him that one day he would inherit it from him.

Sadly, he thought back to it and clasped the watch in his hand and held it to his heart.

"Don't you like her?", irritated, Greta looked at Aiden's behaviour.

Elisabeth jumped up and went to Aiden.

"Will you show me the watch."

She took the pocket watch from his hand and admired the beautiful piece.

"But Greta, where did you get that watch? It's far too valuable." Now Elisabeth was really upset.

"Oh...", Greta waved it off casually. "That's one of many from my uncle. My aunt has a whole jewellery box full of pocket watches. So I thought to myself, I can spare one of them."

Aiden listened silently to the two women.

"But you can also sell them on the black market. Times won't get any better and you'll need every mark," Elisabeth interjected doubtfully.

"Believe me Elisabeth. I have enough. Where do you think I got the meat for our Christmas roast? Don't worry about it. My aunt has left me more than I would ever have guessed. But please don't tell anyone," she winked conspiratorially at Elisabeth.

Elisabeth was very surprised that Greta, of all people, had given Aiden such a precious gift.

When she distrusted him so much. Yes, Greta was simply incomprehensible. Always so impulsive and unpredictable.

Aiden still held the watch in his hand. Could he accept the gift?

But before he could say anything in reply, Greta beat him to it.

"Fritz, not another word. Accept the gift or I'll be offended." And that was the end of the subject for Greta.

"Thank you Greta." said Aiden finally, giving her a smile.

Then he also went out of the room and came back with a small package and handed it to Elisabeth.

"I'm afraid I don't have a present for you, Greta. The time was too short. I didn't know we were going to spend tonight together," Aiden apologised to Greta for not having a present for her.

"It doesn't matter, boy. That's all right."

"Thank you." he replied.

Somehow he was suspicious of the whole situation with Greta.

One time she was totally dismissive and suspicious and then, like today, so over-friendly, almost too pushy.

Until now she had not wanted to have anything to do with him, but today she behaved differently and gave him such a valuable gift. He absolutely had to talk to Elisabeth about it later.

As he looked over at her, he also took in her astonished look and he figured that she was just as puzzled by Greta's behaviour as he was.

"But now open your present from Aiden," Greta prompted Elisabeth, who was still holding the wrapped present in her hands.

Elisabeth opened the gift from Aiden and, completely overwhelmed, held a carved sheep in her hand.

"How beautiful it is. Did you make it yourself?"

Aiden looked at her sheepishly.

"Yes, I did a lot of carving as a child. And on one of our walks I found that piece of wood and took it with me. Do you remember that?"

"Yes, of course. I had already thought what had happened to it. Thank you Fritz."

She looked lovingly at the sheep in her hands. She stood up and put it under the Christmas tree.

Greta watched the scene with interest.

"What makes you think it's a sheep?" she then wanted to know.

"Umm, I like sheep," he replied uncertainly.

Elisabeth saved the situation by getting up and going to the living room cupboard and taking out a liqueur she kept there, as well as three glasses.

"So, now let's have a toast, to the beautiful presents."

The evening was still very harmonious and at half past eleven Greta finally said goodbye tiredly and went back to her flat.

"You did very well, Aiden. Oh, Fritz, I meant to say."

Laughing, she shook her head.

"I guess I'll never get used to calling you Fritz. I hope I don't slip up at some point when Greta is here right now."

"It was a beautiful evening. Thank you Elisabeth, for the book and all you do for me."

Aiden never tired of thanking Elisabeth. He knew what she was putting on the line for him.

"It's all right, my boy," touched, Elisabeth turned to the table and began to clear the glasses.

Aiden helped her and they put everything away in the kitchen.

"Greta is acting very strangely, don't you think? I don't know what to make of it," Aiden remarked.

"Yes that's right Aiden. She has always been so unpredictable and capricious. But it was still a nice evening," Elisabeth replied. "But now let's go to bed. It's getting late."

"May I listen to the song again? «

"Yes, of course. Come, let's sit down for a moment and dedicate the moment to Franz."

After Aiden had placed the tone arm on the record and turned the crank, he sat down with Elisabeth and both listened to the music, each lost in their own thoughts.

Later, when Aiden looked out of the window in his room, he saw thick white fast flakes falling from the sky. He watched the flakes for some time.

In his homeland in Ireland, snow was very rare and when it did fall, it was only for a short time and disappeared again immediately. That's why he had been amazed for weeks that here in Germany snow was already falling in November, so much that within a very short time the streets were covered with a thick white layer.

*

Elisabeth and Aiden spent New Year's Eve alone in the flat. At 12 o'clock, they went to the window and opened it to better hear the bells of the churches ringing in the New Year.

"Here's to a new year, which I hope will soon bring us peace," exclaimed Elisabeth, full of hope.

Aiden looked at her sadly. Did Elisabeth really believe that the war would soon be over, he wondered.

The news in the newspapers continued to report the full commitment of the Central Powers.

Elisabeth explained to him that one should not take everything in the newspapers at face value, as these reports would never reveal the true losses at the front. New propaganda sheets appeared every few weeks to strengthen the stamina of disillusioned citizens and to discourage unrest. These sheets were also sent to the front-line soldiers to motivate them to continue fighting.

In these papers, even defeats were reinterpreted as victories. These propaganda papers were also published in all neutral states such as Italy and the USA, she explained to Aiden.

"How do you know all this, Elisabeth?"

"I have an acquaintance who works in one of these printing houses and who has good contacts with higher authorities. He enlightened me about not being blinded by the propaganda reports and films running in the cinemas. It all has nothing to do with what is really going on at the front."

With a shudder, Aiden thought back to his time at the front. Elisabeth closed the window so that it wouldn't get too cold in the flat and sat down on the sofa with a glass of punch. Aiden remained standing with his back to the window.

"He showed me unofficial pictures that are not supposed to be released to the public."

She drank a few sips of the warm drink before continuing.

"And what can be seen in these pictures is the cruel truth. Even though I still doubted it at the beginning and liked to hear the propaganda reports because they are also reassuring, your description from the front convinced me that everything my acquaintance told me is the truth."

Silently they looked at each other.

"I hope so much that the war will end soon. I hope so much for all of us," Elisabeth whispers sadly.

"Even though the end of the war means that my Franz will not come back, I hope for those who have not yet fallen that they can return to their families."

There was an oppressive silence in the room.

"Well, enough with these horror stories, my boy.

Tomorrow the new year begins and I have my first assignment at the tram depot tomorrow."

*

Elisabeth and Greta had handed in their applications at the Munich tram depot in Lindwurmstraße one day before Christmas and after the Christmas holidays they received the news that Elisabeth as well as Greta would be employed there.

On New Year's Day 1917, they had to report to the main depot for a short training session and were issued with their service uniforms. For the first week they would be escorts to learn the ropes, and from the second week of January they would be main conductors. Elisabeth was very excited, but the much better pay there would help her a lot to feed Aiden and this was a great motivation for her.

*

The next few months passed without anything special happening. Elisabeth went to the tram depot early in the morning, Aiden sat down at the kitchen table after putting away the breakfast dishes and set about his tasks that Elisabeth had given him in the evening, which she had prepared beforehand.

Besides learning vocabulary and grammar, he spoke the words and phrases aloud to himself until he managed to pronounce them without an audible accent.

During the breaks he took, he often stood at the window, behind the curtains, looking down at the street and watching the people hurriedly going their way.

He often fell into sadness when he thought of home, of Ireland.

But he soon chased the thoughts away again and continued to devote himself to his tasks.

He had no choice but to accept the situation as it was, but also to do everything to ensure that he would be perfectly prepared when the time came for him to leave the country., and for that, it was worth doing his best.

By now he had learned to prepare potatoes, cabbage and vegetables or a soup and soon he could expect Elisabeth with the finished meal when she came home from work.

A few times a week, he would walk with Elisabeth to the nearby park in the late evening so he could get some fresh air and get out of the flat.

*

The third month of 1917 dawned.

In March, the days slowly became warmer again as the sun exuded its power and the snow slowly but steadily melted away.

Aiden was increasingly drawn to the outdoors, but still didn't trust himself to go out on the street alone.

The fear of being approached was too great, even though he could already express himself very well.

But more and more, the proverbial ceiling fell on his head and he threatened to fall into a depression.

He was haunted by nightmares about his time at the front. Cruelty struck mercilessly in these dreams.

Almost every day he asked Elisabeth if there was any news about an end to the war.

But Elisabeth could not give him hope, as there was no end to the war in sight.

She had great sympathy for the boy and tried to distract him as best she could when she was at home.

But he simply spent too much time alone in the flat.

Some evenings Greta joined them. More and more he was able to join in the conversations. He thought about every word before saying it out loud so as not to fall into his Irish accent. Since he only spoke German with Elisabeth, his vocabulary was now very extensive.

One day, when the monotony of the flat was particularly upsetting, he cautiously opened the flat door and peered through the crack into the stairwell to see if anyone was there. But everything was quiet.

Therefore, he dared and stepped outside the flat door.

He had put on a grey wool coat that came from Franz and was two sizes too big for him. But he didn't care.

He only wanted to go out the door for a moment. He had clamped the wooden crutches under his arm. They were to serve him to be seen as injured, although he no longer needed them for his leg, because his injury had almost completely healed.

He pulled the flat door shut, putting the key in his trouser pocket.

It was still quiet in the stairwell. Slowly he descended the two floors. Always listening for footsteps or noises.

When he reached the bottom of the stairs and stood in front of the heavy door, it was suddenly pushed open from the outside and the little boy he had met when he arrived stood in front of him. The boy looked at him in amazement.

"You again? Do you live here?" he asked, curious and amazed at the same time.

Aiden remained rooted to the spot.

"Uh....no, yes..... I'm visiting," he finally replied as accent-free as he could. And he managed it well, he thougt to himself in amazement.

"I see. Yes, then. I thought so, because I've seen you on the street a few times with Elisabeth," the boy replied and rushed past him up the stairs.

Aiden looked at him for a moment before opening the front door and stepping outside onto the pavement.

He breathed in the fresh air deeply. The sun shone on his face and warmed him.

A few metres I will walk, he thought to himself.

The crutches in the crooks of his arms, he leaned heavily on them to give the impression that he needed them.

So he limped down the street and went around the whole block.

Carriages drove along the cobbled streets.

and automobiles passed him by. Busy women walked with shopping baskets passed him without noticing him. Other war-disabled persons, like him, limped slowly through the streets.

He felt safer by the minute. The fear faded because he observed that no one really took notice of him and no one cared that he was on the street.

Twice he walked around the block and looked at the houses and the small shops in daylight, as he had only walked along here in the dark so far.

After an hour, he returned to the flat.

When he had closed the door of the flat behind him, the tears welled up in his eyes at the freedom he felt. From now on, he would take a walk in the daylight every day.

First thing in the morning he wanted to go as far as the big park and sit on a park bench there and enjoy nature, the green of the meadow and the trees.

In the evening he excitedly told Elisabeth about his little excursion and his short conversation with the boy who lived in the house.

Elisabeth was surprised and also a little afraid whether it was already reasonable for him to go out alone.

But Aiden reassured her in flawless, accent-free German and she couldn't help but smile at him and give him a hug.

From that day on, Aiden walked for at least two hours every day. Even when it was pouring with rain, he didn't let it stop him, but always making sure he didn't forget to limp.

Elisabeth felt more and more every day that he was beginning to blossom again and she rejoiced with him.

At weekends they went to the park together or they took the tram through the city and she showed him the sights, like the Mariensäule on Marienplatz. She presented him with the Residenz, where Ludwig III lived for a time and was crowned in the throne room in 1913. They strolled down Maximilianstraße to the Maximilianeum, where the student foundation and the royal page school were housed.

Aiden marvelled at the magnificence of the imposing buildings.

He loved these trips to the city, after months spent lonely in the flat.

Every day, during the week, when Elisabeth was at work, he studied throughout the morning, diligently improving his German and pronunciation.

In the afternoon he went to the park and did his rounds there before sitting down on a park bench and thinking of Ireland. Every day he imagined himself there, on the green hills of the Hill of Tara, descending to his parents' little cottage and knocking on the door.

With the image before his eyes, he dreamt of his mother opening the door for him and taking him into her arms. How they would sit in front of the fireplace in the evening and he would tell his story over and over again. Of Franz, who had saved his life, of Elisabeth, who had taken him in unconditionally and walked with him through this difficult time. He imagined that his father would be proud of his son because he had managed to come back to them.

He heard Eimear, his sister, talking and chattering, as she had always done, wanting to know everything about this Germany.

Yes, he lost himself there, in the green park on the park bench in his thoughts, which he decorated with pictures in his mind's eye.

Only rarely did he allow fears to convince him that things might be very different if he ever managed to return home. That perhaps his parents were no longer alive and the cottage would be deserted.

Most of the time, he quickly dispelled these bad thoughts and firmly believed that everything had a good end.

Sometimes he would hold the golden coin he always carried in his hand, holding it tightly in his closed fist, trusting in its destiny that he would always be protected. So far, the coin has kept its promise.

He had to smile when he thought of the legends and sagas of the goblins and fairies in his country. For he knew that they really existed. Even if he thought, as he so often did, that the story he had experienced as a six-year-old child had perhaps only come from his fantasy play, which he had always been only too happy to escape into. But the golden coin in his hand made him believe it, because he wanted to believe it and it gave him hope.

*

It was already mid-May and spring was well on its way.

Aiden went to the English Garden in the afternoon, as he did every day, in the direction of the Chinese Tower.

To do this, he had to walk almost across the entire park.

His distances became longer and longer and he regained more and more strength and power.

When he arrived there, he sat down in the shade of a tree. It was glorious sunny weather and many children were romping around the wooden tower playing tag or hide and seek. Some were put by their parents on the wooden merry-go-round, which went round and round in circles.

The children whooped merrily and pushed their imaginary wooden horses to go faster, which of course did not work.

On the benches around the tower sat mothers or servants with full shopping baskets, exchanging ideas with other servants of the higher-ranking houses and spreading the latest gossip.

Enjoying the sun shining on his face filtered through the foliage of the tree, he sat there when suddenly he heard a woman's voice next to him that sounded familiar.

Surprised, he opened his eyes and saw her right next to him. Anna, the girl he had met at the station when he arrived in Munich. He sat up with a jerk so that his crutches slipped to the grond.

Quickly, the girl bent down picked them up and handed them to Aiden.

"Hello, can you still remember me? We met at the station a few months ago."

It took Aiden a few seconds to tear himself away from those beautiful blue eyes, into which he stared as if spellbound. Her blonde curls fell softly to her narrow shoulders, framing her delicate face with its velvety, slightly golden skin, like a precious painting.

Hastily he stood and put the wooden crutches against the side of the bench before turning back to her and extending his right hand in greeting.

This gave him a few seconds to sort out his words in his mind before pronouncing them without an accent.

"Good day. Yes, I remember you. Of course I do. Anna was your name, wasn't it?"

"You can still remember that? Then you did understand me when I spoke to you. I thought you couldn't hear me and when you didn't answer, I was a bit perplexed."

"I could understand almost nothing. But I understood your name," Aiden replied slowly, his words deliberate. "I just couldn't speak.

I've been painstakingly relearning that for the past few months. So you'll have to forgive my bumpy pronunciation."
"Oh, I thought so, because you speak a bit strangely. How could that happen?" she asked sympathetically but also curiously.
"A cannon hit not far from me. My leg was badly injured and I must have been unconscious for a long time. After that I could no longer hear anything or speak.
The doctors said it was a trauma."
Anna looked at him sympathetically and put a hand on his arm.
"You must have experienced terrible things. Where were you at the front?"
Aiden sat back on the bench and offered Anna the seat next to him. She immediately settled down next to him. She placed her basket on the ground.
"I was in France on the Western Front. More precisely, on the Sommé. The front line runs along this river."
"Your name is Franz, isn't it? I can still remember it." Smiling, she looked at him from the side.
Aiden broke out in a sweat as he remembered that in the distress he was in at the station, he had introduced himself to her as Franz because it was the only word he could pronounce and he couldn't think of any other name.
He feverishly thought about how he could talk his way out of this misery. Elisabeth had given him the name Fritz. He couldn't let this girl believe that his name was Franz.
The confusion would be too much for him in the long run. Embarrassed, he kneaded his hands.
"I guess I told you some nonsense. I wasn't in my right mind.

My uncle's name was Franz and mine is Fritz," Aiden replied apologetically.

He lied to this nice girl only reluctantly. But he had no choice. He hardly knew her and didn't know how she would react if he revealed himself as an Irishman, as an enemy.

"So your name is Fritz, not Franz. Well, hello Fritz.

I am Anna Braun. And what is your last name?"

"Fritz von Letten," he answered hesitantly.

Inside him at that moment a voice screamed his real name, Aiden McGilles, very loudly.

He swallowed the rising panic with difficulty.

For the first time, he realised how difficult it was to come into contact with other people without authentically revealing himself as who he really was. All he carried on the outside were lies about him.

"of Latvians? Really? «

Astonished, she looked at him. "I know a Franz von Letten. He is, or was, a teacher at my school. And I also know his wife Elisabeth, she was one of the first women allowed to teach at the school."

"You went to his school?" replied Aiden.

"Yes, that was me. Is Franz von Letten your father?" asked Anna in amazement.

"No, he was my uncle. My father's brother," he answered quickly.

Elisabeth must have drilled this into his head hundreds of times if anyone were to ask him about his relationship to her and Franz.

"Why was? Is he no longer alive?" She looked at him in dismay.

"Franz unfortunately fell a few months ago." Aiden sadly lowered his gaze.

"Really, my God, how sad." Tears welled up in Anna's eyes. "He was such a nice man. I liked him a lot"

Both remained silent for a while, each absorbed in their own thoughts.

"And your parents? Why aren't you with your mother? Do you still have brothers and sisters?"

Again, Elisabeth had made up a story in case he was asked about it.

"Unfortunately, both my parents are no longer alive. I am the only child. Franz and Elisabeth are my only relatives. I didn't know where else to go after my injury.

That's why I came here to Munich to Elisabeth. I couldn't go back to the front yet, because my leg was still causing too many problems and I had to heal my trauma first. Almost at the same time, Elisabeth learned that Franz, her husband, had been killed." Sadly, he whispered the last words and the memory of his encounter with Franz at the front appeared before his eyes as if it had been only yesterday.

"How sad," Anna whispered.

Again they remain sitting silently next to each other for a while until Anna suddenly lifted the basket from the ground and removed the cloth.

Underneath was a cake, as Aiden recognised from the scent that emanated from the basket.

His mouth watered, suddenly overcome by hunger.

"Would you like a piece of the Gugelhupf?", Anna asked and cut a large piece out of the round cake with a knife that had also been in the basket.

"Yes, with pleasure. Did you bake it yourself?"

"Yes, I did. I wanted my grandmother's cake
and have a coffee with her.
But I'm sure she won't mind if I give you a piece of it."
She handed him a piece of the fragrant cake and he bit into
it with relish. Anna also cut herself a piece and took a
courageous bite.
Suddenly, they both turned their heads towards each other
at the same time and had to laugh as their mouths were
covered in cake crumbs.
They ate the cake with great appetite. And Aiden sat back
with relish.
"bhí sé go maith," it flashed across Aiden's lips, meaning 'was
that good'.
Anna looked at him in amazement.
"What did you say?"
Aiden's pale skin turned deep red and he desperately
searched for words.
"Um... Oh....that just slipped out. Sorry."
Ringing his hands, he sought an explanation for his Irish
words.
"My mother taught me Latin and sometimes I speak like
that," he tried to talk his way out of it, hoping that Anna
didn't know Latin.
The latter, however, looked at him sceptically.
"That wasn't Latin," she said suspiciously. "I can speak and
write some Latin too, but that sounded quite different."
"Then I must have said it wrong. I'm not good at it. I just
wanted to say that the cake tastes good," he tried to find a
plausible explanation for her.
Still sceptical, she looked at him from the side.

But he said nothing more about it and put the knife back in the basket and covered the cake with the cloth.

Strange boy, she thought to herself. But she liked him and felt comfortable in his company.

Well, his way of speaking was quite unique, but she put this down to the fact that he had lost his speech and his hearing and now had to learn everything again with great difficulty.

Anna noticed that Aiden was watching her intently from the side. But when she turned her face to him, he quickly looked away.

Somehow the spell of their getting to know each other was broken. Anna looked very thoughtful.

Aiden felt himself stupid and careless that this had happened to him.

He knew he had to be more careful in the future and not get carried away with feelings of delight and always stay focused when he wasn't alone.

But he hadn't felt as good as he did in Anna's company for a long time. He could have sat with her for hours on this park bench, here in front of the imposing Chinese Tower in the park.

"Will you be here again tomorrow?" asked Anna suddenly.

"Yes, I come here almost every day."

"It's strange that we've never met. I often walk through the park too, usually after lunchtime, but not every day."

"What else do you do? Do you still go to school?" Aiden looked at Anna with interest.

"No, no, I don't go to school anymore. Not for a year.
I went to grammar school and when I was 18, a year ago, I finished school."

"And what are you doing now?"

"I was planning to train as a teacher. But it is very difficult as a woman to be admitted to a university for that. I wanted to go to Heidelberg, where I would have had a better chance. But unfortunately nothing came of it, because my mother fell ill and I had to stay at home and look after her." She looked at Aiden unhappily.

"I'm sorry about that. It must not be easy for you that your mother is ill and you can't realise your plans."

"Yes, it's not easy. But I have to be there for my mother. My father is in the war and I am the only child now. My brother was killed a year ago on the Western Front."

Tears came to her eyes before she continued speaking.

"My grandmother is already too old to take care of my mother."

"What's wrong with your mother?"

"It's hard to say. It's her mind. She just sits there and there is no will to live in her. This has been so since we got the news of my brother's death. It is as if she has been living in another world ever since. My father comes home from the front as often as he can. But she doesn't even notice him when he is there. She only lets me help her eat and go to bed. Otherwise she sits in her chair and stares at herself. We have already taken her to different doctors. But everyone just shakes their heads. They say that she is in a kind of rigor mortis, which might come off at some point."

Despondently she lowered her gaze.

"Alternatively, we could put her in an institution, but my father didn't want that in any case and so I am tied up here and had to give up my plans. Who knows how long the war will last and whether my father will survive it unscathed, which I deeply hope he will.

But then it will be too late for me and I will probably look for a husband and become a wife and mother. It's not the worst thing to do."

Resignedly, she shrugged her shoulders.

Aiden's soul ached when he felt the sadness that gripped Anna. He would have loved to put his arm around her shoulders.

But he did not dare and refrained from this urge. He did not want to offend her.

"But now enough with the lamentations. How old are you? And what did you do before you went to war?"

Again, Aiden felt very pressured, triggered by her questions. What was he supposed to tell Anna? He had learned nothing, only helped his parents in the fields. His father had been a carpenter in earlier years and showed him some of the craft, and he often helped him when he was making a new chair or a table.

"Ohhh...I'm 19 years old and I worked as a carpenter," he then answered quickly and succinctly.

"Carpenter, what a beautiful profession. ", Anna exclaimed delightedly.

Aiden continued.

"But I only worked for my father for a short time, then the war came and father didn't get any more jobs because everyone's money was getting tighter and tighter. We mainly worked our fields and tended the few sheep we owned."

"Sheep? You have sheep at home. No cows or pigs? ", Anna asked curiously.

Aiden felt a chill run down his spine. Had he said something wrong? He didn't know if there were sheep farmers in Germany.

217

Instinctively, he decided to simply stick to the truth in this case.

"Yes we have a whole flock of sheep at home and we sell the wool."

"Oh yes, that's interesting. You'll have to tell me more about that," Anna eyed him curiously.

Aiden shuddered, not knowing what he could and could not say without her becoming suspicious.

Finally, he decided to retreat spontaneously.

"I'm afraid I have to go home now Anna. Elisabeth will be home from work soon." He rose quickly at his words, as if he couldn't wait to say goodbye.

Anna looked up at him in surprise at his sudden departure and then stood up as well.

"I didn't mean to offend you. Sorry for being so nosy."

Aiden stepped sheepishly from one foot to the other. He felt totally overwhelmed by her questions at the moment. He should have discussed these things better with Elisabeth. He really had to make up for it. Tonight he would sit down with Elisabeth and go through all the possible questions he could be asked.

"Don't worry about it. It's okay. I just have to go now."

"Will we see each other again?" Anna looked at him questioningly as he lifted his crutches and tucked them under his armpits.

"Yes, of course, with pleasure. I'll be back tomorrow at the same time," he answered hastily. Because there was nothing he liked better than being in the company of this beautiful girl, despite the many questions she asked.

"Goodbye then and maybe see you tomorrow."

She turned and strolled away with her basket.

"Thank you for the cake. It was really very good," Aiden called after her.

Anna gave him another quick wave before disappearing down the narrow path between the trees.

Aiden also made his way home. A storm of emotions raged inside him. He felt like a fraud, which he kind of was. So much he would like to tell her the truth, about him and his family and everything that had happened. But the danger was just too great and he would only put her in danger with his tall tale. He wanted to avoid that at all costs, in case he was discovered one day and arrested. Inevitably, everyone who knew about the affair would be punished. It was bad enough for him that he could get Elisabeth into big trouble.

*

Once back in the flat, he sat down on the sofa and stretched out his feet.

His thoughts wandered to Anna and his heart warmed when he thought of her smile. Those sweet dimples that appeared on her cheeks when she smiled or laughed.

He would have loved to brush her curls from her face with his hands. Everything about her brought out feelings in him that he had never known.

He had never really been in love before.

Yes, maybe a little, with the sister of his friend from the distant neighbourhood. But that was nothing like what he had just felt here with Anna.

It was as if his soul inside him had called out 'yes' very loudly.

Only now did he consciously think of this loud 'yes' he had heard inside himself. What was it? It felt so full, big and wide inside him.

Stretched out on the sofa, he crossed his arms, grinned to himself and closed his eyes to trace this wonderful feeling.

Finally he had fallen asleep and dreamed of a sweet, blond girl whom he took by the hand and ran with her up the green hills of the Hill of Tara.

Her hair blew in the strong wind that usually blew up there. Once at the top, he let himself fall with her into the lush, dense green of the hills, bent over her and kissed her mouth, the full pink lips that offered themselves to him longingly.

'Anna, Anna, darling, tá tú chomh gleoite. (Darling, you are so sweet)', Aiden whispered, caught up in his sweet dreams.

"Aiden, Aiden!" he heard his name, as if through a veil of mist.

'Anna! Seo anois mé' (here I am), he shouted into this fog-drenched room.

"Aiden, wake up," he heard the energetic voice again.

Only with great difficulty did he free himself from his dream, reluctantly opened his eyes and saw Elisabeth bending over him.

Startled, he pulled up and put his legs on the floor.

Elisabeth looked at him with a smile.

"That must have been a beautiful dream. I only ever heard you call out the name 'Anna'.

I didn't understand the other words. I guess that was Irish?" she looked at him with a wink.

"Yes, that was a nice dream," he replied sheepishly, not knowing whether to tell Elisabeth about his encounter with Anna.

However, before he could finish this thought, Elisabeth began to question him.

"Who is this Anna you were dreaming about?" she looked at Aiden with an expectant smile. "Have you met someone?" she added, but with some concern in her voice.

The danger of Aiden being discovered as a deserter, and from the enemy camp at that, was always lurking. So far, she hadn't had to worry about him because he didn't socialise and spent most of his time indoors. But she had already noticed that he was more and more drawn to the outside. Where danger lurked.

Now the time had come. He had probably met a girl on his daily walks.

"Yes, it's a girl. She knew Franz."

Elisabeth looked at him in dismay.

"And she knows you too. From school, she told me."

"What is this girl's last name?"

"Braun. Anna Braun is her name."

Elisabeth thought for a moment. Then recognition appeared on her face.

"Oh, little Anna. Yes, of course I know her. A very nice girl." Aiden told her about their first meeting at the station and their reunion today in the English Garden.

"So, will you see each other again?"

"Yes, I think so," he replied with a smile.

"Please take good care of yourself. Although I think she could be trusted, we don't want to risk anything."

"I know, Elisabeth. We really need to discuss a few more things about me, otherwise I'll be in hot water. She asked me questions about my family and me that I hadn't expected and

I had to think of something on the fly, which wasn't easy for me."

"I don't know if it's a good idea for you to become close friends with someone," Elisabeth reflected. "But I can understand that you're looking for company. Who knows how long the war will last. It seems like there's no end to it. But promise me you'll be more than careful. It's just too dangerous for you.

Everything would have been for nothing, and I don't want anything to happen to you."

Aiden looked at her dejectedly.

"Yes, I know, Elisabeth. I promise you I will be careful."

"Come on, get up now. We'll eat first and then we'll make you a complete CV, which you can then learn and internalise so that you become more confident in dealing with strangers."

Aiden rose and went with her to the kitchen. Together they prepared dinner and then sat down at the table.

Later, Elisabeth took a sheet of paper out of the drawer and they created a CV for Aiden to use as a guide in the future.

*

The next day, Aiden went to the park again, sat down on the bench and waited for Anna. But when she still hadn't come by after almost two hours, he continued on his way disappointedly before going home again.

This repeated itself over the next few days. He always waited for almost two hours on the bench, at the Chinese Tower, when he found that she did not come he left disappointed and went home.

After a week, he had almost given up hope as he strolled to the park bench. Would he wait in vain again today? Fate probably wanted them not to meet again, or else, Anna did not want to meet him again.

These negative thoughts flashed through his mind, giving him a panicky feeling. If she was deliberately avoiding him, then maybe she didn't like him at all?

Briefly, he sat down on the bench and watched the children running and playing happily around the tower, under the supervision of their mothers, who sat spread out on the benches talking.

After a while he stood up and was about to continue on his way when he suddenly heard someone calling loudly behind him.

"Fritz, Fritz, wait for me."

He turned quickly and saw Anna running towards him. Her cheeks were red from running and she stopped breathlessly in front of him.

"Anna, I didn't even believe I would see you again," he cried with relief.

"I couldn't leave my mother alone for the last few days. She was very unwell and I had to stay with her in the flat," she replied sadly.

"But you're here now. Come, let's sit on the bench." And pointed to the park bench at the side of the path.

As they sat, Anna told him that her mother had tried to take her own life when she was out shopping a few days ago. She was very unwell and had dissolved the whole tube of tablets she was taking for her depression in a glass of water. She got home just in time and was able to prevent something worse.

Aiden took her hands in his and squeezed them sympathetically.

Suddenly Anna burst into tears and leaned her head against his shoulder. He put his arm around her and squeezed her soothingly while her tears flowed.

They sat like that for a while until Anna had calmed down a bit.

"I don't know how to help her. The doctor said we should take her to the psychiatric institution. But I don't want that under any circumstances. She would only be locked up there. I'm sure my father wouldn't allow that under any circumstances.

I have already sent him a letter to the front, but it will probably take him a while to receive it. I don't know what to do," she said desperately.

"Where is your mother now?"

"My grandmother came to look after her while I was out. She said I really needed to get some fresh air. So I thought I'd see if you were here."

"I've been here every day waiting for you," Aiden said quietly.

"I'm sorry about that. But I couldn't notify you."

Silently they sat leaning against each other and enjoyed the closeness.

Suddenly Aiden had an idea.

"Do you think I can visit you at your house too?"

He looked at her with eager anticipation.

Anna lifted her head and looked at him, then shrugged slightly.

"Yes, why not. My mother might not even notice you or she might not care, as apathetic as she is."

"Then I'll visit you tomorrow afternoon. What do you think?"

"Yes, with pleasure. We live at 25 Elisabethstraße, on the second floor. I'll tell my mother that I'm expecting a visitor for tea and then I'll see how she reacts, or if she reacts at all. I'll just tell her that you are an old school friend who has just returned injured from the war. «

"That's what we'll do. And if she does object to my visit, then I'll just leave again so you don't get into trouble."

Anna smiled happily at the prospect of no longer having to spend time alone with her mother in the flat.

Aiden hugged her tightly to his chest again, feeling like a knight holding his princess protectively in his arms.

"Now I have to go and relieve my grandmother," Anna said and stood up with a heavy heart, saying goodbye to Aiden with a long handshake. He reluctantly let go of her hand and held it longer than necessary before she went on her way.

When she had disappeared from his sight, after she had turned around a few times and waved to him, Aiden remained sitting, looking forward like a little boy to seeing Anna again.

His heart leapt and the butterflies in his stomach danced around and gave him a warm feeling.

*

The next afternoon he set off, having put on his best trousers and shirt.

Little by little, Elisabeth had adapted her husband Franz's shirts and trousers to Aiden's measurements and made them smaller. She was very skilled in using the sewing machine.

He combed his reddish-blond hair back neatly and took some pomade to tame the wild strands. His otherwise very fine hair had grown back much thicker at the front after being shaved bald, it was as a neat mane, with light, wavy curls on his head.

When he looked in the mirror in the bathroom, he was pleased with his sight and grinned, full of anticipation in the mirror.

You're acting like an idiot in love, he said to his reflection, but the grin remained on his lips.

Half an hour later, he was standing in front of the flat door on the 2nd floor, at Elisabethstraße 25, pressing the bell above which the name Braun was written in gold letters and dancing around on his crutches with excitement.

Anna opened the door, beaming with joy, and let him enter. Both felt a little uncertain and did not know what to say at first.

But the joy of the reunion was written all over their faces.

"My mother is sitting in the living room," she whispered to him.

"I told her you were coming for tea, but she just looked at me and didn't say anything about it.

So don't be surprised if she doesn't respond to you," she warned him.

Then they entered the living room and Anna went to a large, old wing chair where a gaunt, slumped woman sat. Her pale, grey hair was pulled up into a bun, her grey face was criss-crossed with wrinkles, her eyes, which had surely once shone as blue as Anna's eyes, were watery blue, poking out of their deep-set sockets and staring silently ahead of her.

Her mouth was pinched shut. She wore a black, ankle-length dress that half hid her thin, wrinkled neck.

Her hands clasped together, lay in her lap.

"Mother, this is Fritz," Anna told her gently, pointing at Aiden.

"Good afternoon, Mrs Braun. How are you?"

Aiden stood a little awkwardly in front of the woman and held out his hand to her.

Ilse, Anna's mother's first name, showed no reaction and overlooked Aiden's outstretched hand. Only a very brief, puzzled glance passed over him before she lowered her eyelids again.

"Come Fritz, let's sit down first," Anna urged him.

Aiden still winced inwardly when he was addressed by the name Fritz. Would he ever get used to it?

The desire to tell Anna the truth grew stronger in him every time he was with her.

But never did the right moment arise when he plucked up the courage.

They sat down at the table, which was set with a colourful tea service. In the middle of the table was a cake, already cut into large pieces.

"Mother, will you join us at the table too?"

Anna knelt in front of the wing chair and grabbed her mother by the folded hands. But she did not react, only lowered her head deeper onto her chest and closed her eyes.

Anna stood up and shrugged helplessly before joining Aiden back at the table and pouring the tea.

"Is she always in this state?" whispered Aiden.

"Yes, most of the time.

Very rarely she has lighter moments. Then she also speaks a few words.

But that happens very rarely. My father was at home for a fortnight two months ago. Not even with him did she respond. My grandmother always tries to get her out of this rigidity with loud words and shaking. But that is no use either. The doctors said we have to have a lot of patience."

"I'm very sorry about that, Anna."

"If only I could get her to take a little walk with me so she could get out of the flat. Maybe that would help a little. But she can't be made to do that."

Aiden stayed with Anna for over two hours and they talked quietly before he said goodbye with a heavy heart and went home.

But not before he had promised Anna to come back the next day.

And so it came about that every afternoon Aiden had two, three hours with Anna and they enjoyed being together very much, even if the circumstances were sad.

When Anna's grandmother was in the flat, they went for a walk in the park, otherwise they sat at the living room table. They never ran out of things to talk about and when there were silent moments, they looked deep into each other's eyes and smiled at each other.

Anna blossomed in his company and was thus better able to bear and accept her mother's suffering.

Some days he racked his brains over how to get out of this messy situation. If only this war would finally come to an end.

Elisabeth had gotten him papers to confirm his new identity.

Aiden was so grateful to her for everything she had done for him so far. And when the war was over, he could return to Ireland, to his family, to his home. This was his goal.

Perhaps he could persuade Elisabeth to accompany him. That would be his greatest wish.

But the more time he spent with Anna, the harder he liked the idea of having to leave her too. And he resolved again and again to tell her the truth.

*

So the weeks and months passed and the calendar already showed the beginning of July 1917. The summer was unusually warm.

Some afternoons, when they could leave the flat, Aiden and Anna would lie on a blanket they had brought with them in the park and enjoy their time together.

There were days when they were exuberant, like little children, and Aiden put Anna on the carousel with the wood-carved animal figures, by the Chinese Tower.

Anna told him that the building had been rebuilt and put back into use in 1913 after the previous one had burnt down. Music streamed from the roller organ as soon as the carousel spun and Anna sat on a horse and laughed happily while Aiden stood next to her and did the rounds with her.

These were very special moments they spent together, forgetting everything else around them.

*

Aiden spent his evenings with Elisabeth, who tirelessly continued to teach him German and writing.

Over time, he found great pleasure in writing. For Anna he now often wrote short poems and secretly he had begun to write a love story. He used the feelings he had for Anna, which were growing stronger and stronger, as a model.

So far, he had not dared to come closer to her and to kiss her. Although he often had the feeling that she was just waiting for it.

This showed when he sometimes put his arm around her and pulled her to his shoulder when she was sad. Then she would raise her pretty face to him and look at him with a strange look that almost drove Aiden out of his mind. But quickly he always turned his head away and let her go. A strange shyness gripped him every time he had the opportunity to get so close to Anna.

Later, when he remembered it, he called himself a coward and he got angry with himself.

Elisabeth observed Aiden's relationship with Anna with mixed feelings. She liked the girl very much, but it was difficult to decide whether to include Anna in the secret.

She often talked to Aiden about it, but again and again they came to no conclusion.

Aiden for the reason that he feared for the love that bound him to Anna.

He was very afraid that she would reject him and push him away when she found out who he really was. But he did not believe that Anna would betray him.

No, she would never do that, he was sure of it.

But Elisabeth seemed to have her doubts about this.

You couldn't trust anyone in those times, she used to say.
Aiden felt guilty towards Elisabeth, because if her doubts were justified, he would get her into a lot of trouble.
These were two huge reasons why he had remained silent until now.

*

Summer showed itself from its most beautiful side. August was just as hot as July and people were drawn outside to the cool, tree-lined parks.
An end to the war was still not in sight.
Anna's mother's condition was getting worse and she was very worried. So Aiden now spent every afternoon with Anna and her mother in their flat, keeping her company, and soon they were inseparable.
One evening, while he was having dinner with Elisabeth, the doorbell rang.
Elisabeth stood up and opened the door.
Greta stood in front of the door, completely distraught. It was very rare that she came to visit. Greta had a new boyfriend for some time and spent a lot of time with him. Elisabeth was glad that Greta was distracted and didn't always inquire how long Fritz would be staying with her or why he still hadn't been called back to the front. She remained very suspicious of Aiden all the time and that worried Elisabeth a lot. She knew Greta's stubbornness and mistrust.
Now she was standing in front of the door and wanted to be let in. Elisabeth saw that her eyes were red and she looked very pale and tired.

"Greta, what do you look like? What happened?" Elisabeth asked worriedly.

"May I come in?"

"Yes, of course," Elisabeth replied, albeit somewhat hesitantly, and opened the door fully to invite Greta in.

She stepped into the hallway and immediately burst into tears.

"What happened?" asked Elisabeth in dismay, grasping her gently by the shoulders. "But first come inside."

She took the wine bottle from Greta's hand, which she was clutching tightly to her heart, and led her into the living room.

Aiden sat at the dining table and stared in amazement at Greta, who still crying stepped into the room behind Elisabeth and now looked at Aiden aghast.

"I'll leave you to it then," Aiden said uncertainly, getting up and going to his room.

"Greta, now tell me what happened."

Worried, she pushed Greta to the sofa and they sat down.

Again she burst into tears and Elisabeth let her cry and waited until she had calmed down a little.

"You still let the boy live with you? Doesn't he still have to go back to the front?" were the first words Greta addressed to her.

Elisabeth looked at her in irritation.

"Yes, he will stay with me for as long as necessary and I will do everything I can so that he doesn't have to go back to the front. I've told you that many times.", she answered evasively. "But now tell me what's wrong with you?"

Completely distraught, Greta began to speak while sobbing.

"Anton has been called up to the front again."

Another stream of tears poured down Greta's face.

"It's so unfair. He still has big problems with his hand, which is still stiff and he can't move it properly. He had already served two years at the front before he was wounded.

He was already exempted and employed in the machine factory that manufactures parts for the rifle armour.

I don´t understand? Why did they bring him back to the front? " She clapped her hands over her face, sobbing.

"I don't understand," she repeated. "Anton did the day before yesterday received the position order, and has hardly been since then approachable. We hardly spoke a word to each other. He started by train this morning."

"Oh Greta, I'm so sorry," Elisabeth replied in shock.

Her boyfriend, Anton, did Greta so much good. At last she seemed to have found the man she had always wanted. Even his injury, that he had a crippled hand, had not bothered her at all.

At one point she even let it be known to Elisabeth that they wanted to marry as soon as the war was over.

Elisabeth got up and opened the bottle of wine, poured two glasses full and sat down again with Greta on the sofa and handed her a glass.

"Come on, have a drink first."

"Thank you Elisabeth."

Greta took the glass and drank a big gulp.

"I just can't understand it. When will this war finally end? I can't believe he has gone back to the front. Supposedly they need every man to do relief work.

Anton couldn't tell me what that meant. I don't think he knew exactly himself."

Elisabeth laid her hand comfortingly on Greta's shoulder.
"But then he is protected at least as far as he doesn't have to
go on the battlefield. And has a very good chance of survival,
don't you think?"
Greta shrugged her shoulder despondently and took another
big sip from her glass.
"So much can happen. No one is safe there at the front. And
Anton knows what's coming, which makes it even worse.
He doesn't say much, but he spoke of the hell on earth he
had experienced there. And he was so grateful that it was
over for him. He gladly accepted his crippled hand for that,
as he said. Oh, it's so terrible and so unjust."
Shaking her head, she stares at the heavy crystal glass she
held in her hands.
"There is nothing fair about this war, Greta. Each and every
one of us is exposed to it and has to endure its fate."
"I'm sorry Elisabeth, I know what you've been through in
the last few months. And I am infinitely sorry that your
Franz fell."
"It's all right, Greta. I wish for you, for both of you, that
Anton comes home safely. I ask you to pray for him and I
will do the same."
"Thank you Elisabeth, you are right. I'll try."
She drank another big gulp of wine until the glass was empty.
Suddenly, however, she burst into hysterical crying again.
"I don't want that. I want Anton to be here with me and
I don't have to be afraid for him. What am I going to do? My
thoughts won't stop spinning and the fear almost kills me."
Elisabeth knew Greta very well and knew that she could be
very difficult and self-centred.

Her mood sometimes changed uncontrollably in a matter of seconds.

Elisabeth could remember, when she herself was desperately sad when Franz had to go to war, that Greta had said to her emotionlessly and rationally, *This is a war for our fatherland and that's why our men have to go into battle.*

So Greta had a clear opinion and evaluation for everything that did not concern herself.

But as it was now, her situation, when she was equally affected, everything was unjust and bad.

Elisabeth knew Greta's volatility only too well and she almost had to control herself not to give her a good talking to. But this was not the right moment.

"You have no choice, Greta. You have to come to terms with it, as we all had to do and still have to do," she replied in a controlled manner, although she was not as calm inside as she pretended on the outside.

"Accept? Resign. I don't want to resign.", almost screaming, she uttered the words. "I only have to resign myself when Anton is dead. «

Upset, she jumped up and went to the dining table to pour herself some more wine.

Suddenly she turned around to Elisabeth with a jerk.

"What's actually going on with Fritz. Why wasn't he called up again? Did you have a hand in that?

Do you perhaps have connections to certain places that you haven't told me about?"

Outraged, Elisabeth also jumped up from the sofa.

"Greta, what are you talking about. I have no connections that could prevent your Anton from having to go to the front.

Fritz's leg hasn't healed yet and he still has to walk on crutches, as you saw."

Inside Elisabeth was now seething.

How dare Greta blame her or Aiden for her Anton having to go to the front.

However, Greta was so enraged that she could no longer control herself.

"You don't believe that yourself. I've seen him walk down the stairs in the stairwell a few times without any effort. He didn't need crutches for that."

She angrily threw these words at Elisabeth's feet.

"I knew from the beginning that there was something wrong with this boy. Why are you hiding him here in the flat?"

Elisabeth had to control herself incredibly well not to lose her nerve and yell at Greta as much as she did. But she knew she had to stay calm and not say anything rash that could somehow endanger Aiden.

"Greta, I don't talk to you like that and I forbid you to talk to me like that. You are selfish and defiant, like a little child who doesn't get what she wants. Now control yourself. I understand your pain too well, believe me.

But we are all in the same boat and share the same fate. Your Anton hasn't died yet and he has a good chance of surviving this time at the front."

"Now don't keep deflecting, Elisabeth," Greta shouted back in a hysterically louder voice. "You just don't want to tell me why you're still hiding Fritz in your flat."

"I am not hiding him. He goes outside alone every day, runs errands and soon he will also have a job and so continue to serve the war effort as far as it is possible for him.

He had a lot of trauma to deal with, couldn't hear or speak and had to learn it all again. But you know all that. And I don't have to justify who I take into my home."

Elisabeth was shocked at how much of an argument had just been sparked here with Greta.

She knew this was very dangerous territory. For Greta was unpredictable in her anger and hatred. And they, Elisabeth and Aiden, truly had something to hide.

Greta was very suspicious at first, but for a long time, until now, it was no longer an issue between them. Now, because of this incident, that something in Greta's life was not going the way she thought it would, she was lashing out and looking for someone to blame and someone to take her anger out on.

"No, you can't justify him being able to stay at home while my Anton had to go," Greta blustered at her. "But there's something fishy about this story with your Fritz.

I think you do have connections in the top ranks and you just don't want to help me and Anton, you just want to save this boy's butt."

Greta became more and more abusive. Elisabeth had often seen her angry, but so far others had always been the cause and victims of her aggressiveness.

Elisabeth would have liked to throw her out of the flat. But an inner voice told her not to provoke Greta any more.

There was too much at stake for her and Aiden.

Greta was capable of anything and it would be terrible if she delivered Aiden to the authorities through such a useless argument.

She couldn't confess to her that Aiden would never receive another posting order because he was undeclared and had gone into hiding as an enemy here in Germany, with her.

"Greta, calm down now. There's no point to any of this. Don't blame others for Anton being drafted again," she tried to calm Greta down.

"I don't need to calm down. How could I? It's all so unfair," she repeated to herself. "I suppose I'd better go now. If you decide you do want to help me so Anton can come back, you can get in touch with me."

Enraged, she emptied her glass, crossed the living room, grabbed her coat in the hallway, yanked open the flat door and slammed it loudly behind her.

Elisabeth took a deep breath before she leaned on the table with one hand, exhausted and trembling.

At that moment, Aiden poked his head through the door and looked at Elisabeth in amazement.

"What was that?"

Dismayed, he went to Elisabeth.

"Why did Greta scream so loudly?"

It took Elisabeth a while before she began her report. She didn't want to worry Aiden in any way, but they had to be on their guard. If Greta did not calm down, he was in great danger. Once the authorities put him under the microscope, their secret would blow up in their faces. Perhaps even the false papers would not stand up to that.

Aiden listened to her, startled. He had been listening at the door, but had not understood many of the words in the hectic exchange.

"I think it would be better if I got out of here. I certainly don't want you to get into trouble. You have helped me for so long, but now it will be too dangerous."

"No, absolutely not Aiden," cried Elisabeth firmly. "We'll wait and see for now. I will go up to Greta tomorrow and see if she has calmed down. This is the first shock now, and she is expressing anger and aggression. We've known each other for so long and she won't do anything that could harm me," Elisabeth said, trying not to let her doubts show.

This war corrupts so many people. You could no longer trust anyone.

*

When Elisabeth came home the next evening, she told Aiden that Greta had not exchanged a word with her when they had met at the tram depot to go on duty.

After dinner, Elisabeth made her way to Greta's flat with a queasy feeling. She wanted to talk to her again in private.

Aiden watched her anxiously as she closed the flat door behind her.

Anna came to his mind. He had been with her in the afternoon and anxiously saw how her mother's condition was deteriorating every day.

Meanwhile, she lay in bed all day and was no longer able to sit down in her recliner in the living room.

Every few days the doctor came by, but he too shook his head hopelessly.

Anna told him that the doctor had explained to her that her mother simply didn't want to live any more. That she had given up.

Anna lay crying in his arms.

She hoped so much that her father would come home soon, but still she had not received a reply to her last letter from him.

Still lost in thoughts of the afternoon, he heard the flat door being unlocked.

He hurriedly got up and ran into the hallway. Elisabeth just came in and looked at Aiden dejectedly.

"She couldn't be calmed down. She's really stuck in her anger and despair and doesn't want to see me anymore because I'm not helping her like I'm helping you, she said."

Elisabeth went into the kitchen and made tea. After she returned with two steaming cups, which she placed on the dining table, they sat down in silence.

Aiden stirred thoughtfully in his cup.

"It would be better if I disappeared from here. It will be too dangerous for you if there is a possibility that Greta will turn us in to the authorities," he told Elisabeth his thoughts.

"No, absolutely not, Aiden. Where are you going?"

"I'll find a solution. Better I go underground before we both get locked up."

"Now slow down Aiden. Let's not get ahead of ourselves."

But Aiden jumped up from the chair excitedly.

"Elisabeth, I don't want you to be punished because of me. You have already done so much for me. I don't want to burden you any more than I already have. «

"You're not burdening me, Aiden," she cried desperately.

"I did it with pleasure and I still do it. You were the last person to see and speak to my Franz alive. It was his last wish that I would help you.

He wanted to make it possible for you to survive.

I am also doing this out of love for my Franz. I know that he will watch over us from up there, from heaven. Everything has gone well so far and we will continue to do so until this miserable war is over." With her last words, she desperately tried to suppress the tears that were welling up inside her.

Aiden ran to her and knelt down in front of her and took her hand. Elisabeth motherly put her other hand on his head and tenderly stroked his shock of reddish-blond hair.

"I'm so sorry, Elisabeth."

"You have nothing to be sorry for, Aiden. I will speak to her again. She'll come to her senses," she said in a firm voice. "I will think of something. Remember your golden coin." she tried to cheer him up. "It helped you out of that hopeless situation at the front and will continue to do so. Faith moves mountains, as we say. You'll see."

She still stroked his head soothingly and deep love filled her soul, giving her courage. She stood up and took Aiden in her arms.

"But now I have to go to bed. I am exhausted. "She said and turned around.

She had to be alone and think of something. Somehow she had to manage to calm Greta down again.

*

Munich
September 1917

September arrived. The days became shorter and the air cooler. Elisabeth and Aiden spent the last few weeks very tense. Aiden expected the doorbell to ring at any moment and someone to be at the door to arrest him.

Almost exactly a year ago, he met Franz on the battlefield in France. Now, on his birthday in a few days, it was the anniversary of the beginning of the unusual path he had taken.

He didn't mention anything about the incident with Greta to Anna. What could he say to her? He was always torn between confessing the truth to her.

He became more and more introverted and Anna took him by the arm one afternoon when he was sitting on the sofa with her and looked at him questioningly.

"What's wrong with you Fritz? You've been so quiet for a while."

Aiden didn't know what to say to her.

"Nothing's wrong, Anna. Don't worry," he tried to reassure her and put on a tense smile.

Anna looked at him thoughtfully, then nuzzled her head against his shoulder and snuggled up to him.

So far, they had never gone further than cuddling up to each other, hugging, holding hands and talking. They were very familiar with each other, but nothing more had happened so far.

Anna loved it when she sat next to him like this. She felt safe for those few moments and arrived in infinite proximity to him.

He was her angel, her source of strength during this difficult time she spent caring for and worrying about her mother.

His presence compensated and comforted her for having to abandon all her plans to study to become a teacher.

And now they were sitting there cuddled up close again and she wished he would kiss her.

Courageously, she lifted her face up to him and looked at him.

"You would tell me if something was bothering you, wouldn't you?", Anna looked at him questioningly.

"Of course Anna. It's really nothing."

"If the situation here with my mother is crushing you, you need to tell me."

"No Anna, I really don't."

"Or if it's too much for you to come over every day? It would be fine if you want to spend your afternoons somewhere else."

"Anna, no. There is nothing better for me than spending the afternoons with you",

"Really?" she looked at him sceptically.

"Yes, really. Don't worry"

He hugged her tightly and gave her a kiss on her blonde curly hair, the scent of which he loved.

Expectantly, she lifted her face once more and the tips of their noses touched very gently.

Both remained in this closeness, which suddenly turned into excited tension.

Both could not turn away from each other, both wanted this moment, this feeling, to never end.

Anna closed her eyes and waited eagerly for what was to come now, what she longed for.

Aiden hesitated only a small moment, then he lowered his lips to her slightly open, expectant mouth. Their lips met and it was as if a light ignited in their hearts.

They moved away from each other for a few centimetres and looked into each other's eyes before his lips reunited with hers.

At first it was a small flame, but it ignited more and more every second and became a bright, blazing light, full of passion, the longer they could not let go of each other.

Aiden wrapped his arms around her body and Anna let herself fall in and be carried by him, from cloud to cloud.

Neither spoke a word, as no words were needed to make this moment complete.

Anna was floating in unimagined feelings. This was her first real kiss. And she knew in her heart that it was exactly the right man she was granting it to.

She wanted it to never end and completely lost consciousness of space and time.

Suddenly they were jolted out of their stupor by a scream.

Anna startled and jumped up from the sofa.

"Mum," she cried fearfully and rushed out of the room to join her mother in the bedroom.

Aiden rushed after her. When he arrived in the bedroom, he saw Anna kneeling beside her mother, who had fallen out of bed and was lying on the floor whimpering.

"Mum, what happened?" cried Anna desperately.

"I'll get the doctor," Aiden called out.

"Wait, first we'll put her back on the bed," Anna replied in a panic.

Aiden came closer and gently took Anna's mother under her shoulders and Anna grabbed her feet.

With difficulty they lifted the still whimpering woman onto the bed. Anna sat down with her and stroked her damp forehead desperately.

"I'll run and get the doctor. Do you need anything else that I should bring you?"

"No, I'll wait here. Please hurry."

Aiden rushed out of the flat and ran two streets away, where Doctor Schneider's practice was located.

It took him almost half an hour to arrive back at the flat in Elisabethstraße with the doctor in tow.

After the doctor had examined Anna's mother, he joined them in the living room.

"What's wrong with her? She has always been very apathetic and almost motionless in bed until now."

"Anna, you have to be very strong now. Your mother is coming to the end. This is the last battle she is fighting with herself inside and it can happen that she lashes out. Her spirit is fighting back and doesn't want to leave. You have to be careful now and try to keep her calm so that she doesn't fall out of bed again. I'm sure it will take a few more hours until she calms down and can then leave."

Anna cupped her hands over her face in tears before rushing to her mother's bedside and taking her hand.

"Mum, you can't go now. Daddy will be home soon. You have to wait for him," she cried heartbreakingly and in tears. But her mother could no longer hear her words. She was already in the last throes of death and tossed and turned restlessly.

The doctor stepped into the hallway with Aiden.

"Can you stay with Anna? It may take all night."

"Of course I will stay. Maybe we should inform Anna's grandmother. Surely she would also like to hold the wake with her daughter?" he looked at the doctor questioningly.

"I can let her know. She doesn't live too far from me."

"Thank you very much, Doctor Schneider. Is there anything else we can do to make it a little easier for her?"

"Stay with her and support Anna. Please let me know in the morning how she got through the night. If she makes it through," he added hopelessly.

"Yes, I will do that. Thank you again."

Aiden walked the doctor to the door and they said goodbye to each other.

The doctor turned around once more before stepping out of the door.

"What is your relationship to the Braun family? You were here many times when I visited Mrs. Braun," he looked at Aiden with interest.

"Ohhh... I'm a friend of Anna's," he then answered quite honestly.

"Oh, then you're not a closer relative of the family?"

"No.", Aiden answered truthfully and slightly embarrassed.

"Then it's probably better if the grandmother comes right away. It wouldn't be proper for a strange young man to spend the whole night alone with Anna here in the flat."

He looked sternly at Aiden and walked away.

Aiden looked after him in irritation. What was the doctor actually thinking? That he would seduce Anna the night her mother died next door?

Aiden couldn't believe it. He should leave now? No, he certainly wouldn't. He wanted to stand by Anna and by no means leave her alone.

He closed the flat door and went into the living room.

It was already almost 5 o'clock in the afternoon. Actually, he had to go home. Elisabeth will be worried if he stayed away without letting her know.

He would quickly run to Elisabeth when Anna's grandmother was here and explain everything to her and then come back.

When he returned to the bedroom, Anna was still sitting by her mother's bed and holding her hand, but she kept snatching it away from her, flailing and tossing wildly.

Anna tried to hold her in tears and calm her down, but she only succeeded with difficulty.

Aiden went to Anna and put a hand on her shoulder reassuringly. Anna looked up at him with a tear-stained face. Less than two hours ago, they had shared the most beautiful moment they could have together.

could experience. Now everything was as if extinguished and far away.

But she was so grateful that Aiden stayed here with her.

At that moment, he leaned down and kissed her on her blonde curls, nuzzling his cheek into her hair soothingly.

"I'll stay here with you tonight and stand by you and your mother if that's what you want?" he whispered into her hair.

Anna looked up at him gratefully.

"Yes, stay here. I need you. I don't know where my head is. I can't understand it. I knew she wasn't well, but I never thought she was about to die. What should I do?"

247

"Doctor Schneider sent for your grandmother to come too.
Maybe you have a candle we can light?"
"Yes, of course. Can you please look in the last drawer in the
tall cupboard in the kitchen? There should be candles there
and also matches."
Aiden went into the kitchen and looked for the candles.
He placed two candles on the bedside table and lit them.
Anna was still sitting motionless by the bed and kept holding
her mother's arms and legs when she began to flail wildly.
"When your grandmother is here, I will go to Elisabeth and
let her know that I am keeping vigil with you."
"Thank you Fritz." She looked at him gratefully.
Aiden went into the kitchen and made a pot of tea and some
sandwiches with butter and jam.
He took both into the bedroom.
"Come, have some hot tea," he offered Anna anxiously.

*

The memory of when his grandfather had died a long time
ago came back to Aiden. He himself was four years old at
the time. He remembered how surreal it all was for him, what
was happening in the little cottage where everything was
being witnessed.
The grandfather was lying in the small room that later
became his room. His father sat by his bed and wiped his
forehead with a damp cloth. As his mother told him later,
the grandfather was suffering from a high fever.
A week later he had died. Aiden had watched everything that
happened.

He could remember that his mother had always made tea and lovingly looked after her husband while he kept watch at his father's bedside. The two were very close. And although it was the women's job to look after the old and the sick, his father took on this task as a matter of course, to pay his last respects to his father, to talk to him about things when he had lucid moments that were never spoken before. He wanted to give something back to his father with love and to stand by him in his last hours.

Aiden remembered all that now and he tried to be there for Anna in the same way he had watched his mother.

*

Anna took a few sips of tea, but she refused the sandwiches. Aiden put the plate on the bedside table, ready to hand.

After another half hour, they heard the flat door being unlocked.

Anna's grandmother rushed into the bedroom and to her daughter lying in bed.

"What happened? Doctor Schneider gave me the message to come here quickly because Ilse is very serious," she looked down in dismay at her daughter, who was still tossing and turning very restlessly.

"Mum is going to die, grandmother," Anna whispered in a tear-stained voice.

Reluctantly, Anna rose and let her grandmother take her place at her dying daughter's side.

She sat down and stroked her daughter's face, which was consumed in agony, weeping.

"I saw it coming. She was deteriorating more and more. She gave herself up. My girl, I am here, your mother." She bent close to her daughter and spoke softly to her.

Anna took Aiden by the hand and led him out of the room. "Let's leave her alone with her for a moment so she can say goodbye."

In the living room, they sat down on the sofa where she had received her first kiss just a few hours ago and she was so happy.

She pulled Aiden down to her, leaned against his shoulder and cried softly to herself.

An hour later, Aiden rushed to Elisabeth's in Agnes Street, who was already beside herself with worry because he did not come home. He told her briefly what had happened and that he would stay all night with Anna and her dying mother. Elisabeth hugged him with compassion and let him go again after a few minutes. Aiden didn't want to leave Anna alone for a minute longer than necessary.

In the early hours of the morning, Anna's mother took her last breaths and finally fell asleep.

After a few hours of holding a wake at the deceased's home, Aiden went to fetch Doctor Schneider, who issued the death certificate.

Anna and her grandmother washed the deceased and kept her in bed. However, they could not leave her in the flat for long.

Even now in late summer it was still very warm and therefore necessary to organise the funeral as soon as possible.

Anna sat down at the kitchen table in the afternoon and wrote a letter to her father.

She knew that he would only receive the letter when the funeral, which would take place three days later, would already be over.

Aiden stayed with Anna most of the time and helped her as much as he could with the preparations. Anna did everything as if in a trance.

Sometimes, when her grandmother was not present, she would snuggle up to Aiden and cry silently to herself.

The prayer and the funeral took place quietly. Only a few acquaintances were present.

Anna was incredibly strong and stood by her grandmother, who still could not believe that her daughter had now gone before her.

*

Three weeks later, Anna's father came home from the front. When he received the letter from his daughter, he immediately set off.

Aiden now withdrew a little and let Anna be with her father, which was very difficult for him. He would prefer not to leave Anna alone for a second. But he respected the fact that he was not part of the family.

Only now, after spending his evenings with Elisabeth again, did he tell her the details of what had happened and also that he had fallen madly in love with Anna.

Elisabeth looked at him worriedly.

"You know this has no future Aiden?"

"Yes, Elisabeth, I know. But I can't fight my feelings. What am I going to do?" Sheer desperation was written all over his face.

"I don't know Aiden. We can't take any chances though. Greta is still very aggressive towards me."

In all this time he had spent with Anna, Aiden had not given any more thought to the matter of Greta. He asked Elisabeth if she had repeated her threats again.

Elisabeth told him that Greta no longer exchanged a sensible word with her.

They both hoped that Greta would calm down and that her groom Anton would return home from the front unscathed. But Elisabeth did not trust the peace. She knew Greta, and the way she behaved towards her, nothing was at peace here. She did not share her concern with Aiden, however, because she did not want to worry him further.

Anna's father stayed for a week before he had to return to the front.

With a heavy heart, he left his daughter alone in her grief for her mother. He, too, could hardly bear the grief for his wife. He had not yet been able to come to terms with the loss of his son.

But the hard times at the front did not allow for feelings and emotions. And so he repressed everything heavy that was inside him as best he could. At some moments, he felt as if he were being overpowered by emotion and his insides became rigid and hard as stone so that he could barely endure it.

Now he had to go back, the war knew no sorrow and showed no mercy.

Anna and Aiden accompanied their father to the station and Anna said goodbye in tears.

"Fritz, take good care of my girl," he asked Aiden. "Though it is not fitting that you should spend so much time alone with her, I am glad she has you.

When I get back, we'll talk about your intentions, if you have any towards her. And I entrust her to you now, and I hope you won't disappoint me and be honourable and respectful towards her."

He looked at Aiden urgently.

"Dad, I can take care of myself quite well. You don't have to worry about me.

But I'm glad Fritz is with me and I can always ask him for advice when I'm stuck."

"I have left some money for you on the kitchen table. I don't know how long it will last. But you can always go to your grandmother, you know that."

"I told you I was going to get a job, Dad. Don't worry."

She hugged him again before he boarded the train, waved to them once more and then disappeared into the corridors of the compartments.

Sadly, Anna looked after him. Even when she could no longer see him, she did not avert her gaze.

Aiden waited with her until the train slowly started moving. Then they made their way home. Anna wanted to walk home and slowly they strolled along the streets until they were in Elisabethstraße, in front of Anna's flat.

"Are you still coming up?" she looked at Aiden pleadingly.

"If you still want me with you, I'll be happy to come," Aiden replied.

After a cup of tea and sandwiches that Anna had prepared, they sat wordlessly at the table and looked at each other.

"What do you want to do now, Anna?"

"I have to get a job."

"I could ask Elisabeth if she could put you forward at the tram depot.

They are always looking for people there."

Anna shrugged her shoulders dejectedly.

"My grandmother said that at the Hofbräuhaus, in the City centre, are still looking for waitresses. I'll go there tomorrow and introduce myself. With the tips, you can earn quite well there."

Aiden looked at her sceptically.

He didn't like to imagine Anna struggling with mugs of beer and plates of food.

Aiden had only ever known the Hofbräuhaus from Elisabeth's stories. Whenever she taught Aiden German, she also gave him a detailed description of the city of Munich.

By now he knew everything there was to see and do in Munich in terms of sights and culture, albeit mainly in a theoretical sense. He was also already familiar with Munich's history and it almost felt to him as if he had been born here.

"Let's talk about it tomorrow. I don't want to think about anything now and I'm tired," Anna pulled him out of his thoughts, stood up and held out her hand to him.

"Come on, let's sit on the sofa for a bit."

Aiden followed her and snuggled close they sat in silence for a while.

Suddenly Anna lifted her face up to him and looked at him.

"Please kiss me, Fritz."

Aiden looked at her in amazement. They had not been close and so intimate since the evening her mother had passed away. He had often thought back to that moment almost four weeks ago and dreamt of it happening again.

Slowly he lowered his face towards hers and gently brushed her lips with his.

They remained like that for a few minutes.

Again and again they caressed each other with their lips.

Anna kept her eyes closed, Aiden watching her as she let herself fall and enjoyed the gentle touch.

He felt it was not the time for passion and wild excitement.

He stroked her cheek gently with his hand before leaving her on it.

Anna immediately nestled into his warm hand and kissed his palm lightly and contemplatively.

A pleasant shiver ran through Aiden's body and he closed his eyes as well.

So they sat there and explored each other cautiously, albeit still very shyly and sensitively.

Aiden gently let his hands glide over her body. He stroked her arms with his hands while he continued to nibble gently on her lips. Anna enjoyed the touch and snuggled closer to him.

His hands grew bolder and now gently stroked the rough, black fabric of her blouse and, breathing heavily, he let her lie on her small firm breast, which he felt under the fabric.

He held his hands still, waiting, because he didn't know how she would react to this very intimate touch. But Anna pressed herself even closer to him and let him.

Suddenly she raised her eyes to him.

"May I take your shirt off and touch your skin." She looked at him shyly.

Aiden nodded and helped her unbutton the buttons of his blue and white striped shirt.

Slipping off his sleeves first, he slipped off his shirt after taking his braces off his shoulders. He wore nothing under the shirt as it was very warm that day.

Anna put her cheek against his bare chest and stroked his skin with her hand and closed her eyes again.

Aiden put his head back and tried to cope with his excitement that was overtaking him.

So they lay together in silence for a while until Aiden felt Anna become very still. He looked at her face, which lay motionless on his chest, and realised that she had fallen asleep.

He sat very still and stroked her blond hair. How much he enjoyed this closeness to her and he no longer felt insecure at all about his first experience with a woman. He felt that he only had to follow his feeling.

His thoughts drifted and he thought of home, of his family. Images appeared before his eyes of him standing in front of his parents' cottage with Anna by the hand and knocking on the door. How his mother opened the door and he will sink into her arms and then introduce Anna to her.

He saw his father and sister come to the door because they had heard his familiar voice and they were all in each other's arms, crying with happiness at being reunited.

In the midst of them was his Anna, with whom he then climbed the hills of the Hill of Tara and showed her his land. That was in his thoughts at the moment when Anna had fallen asleep cuddled up to him full of trust.

He felt her body relax more and more in his arms and he remembered a story that his mother had often read to them. It was the story of two lovers who had miraculously met and soon realised that they were two halves of one soul who had found each other again after many years apart.

And the task of the two was that they should heal each other, from fears and from many inner hurts they had to experience on their long, separate journey.

His mother told him that this could be the story of our father and her. That is why she loved this story. She told us that if we meet the second half of our soul one day, we will feel it and know it.

Aiden wondered if Anna was his second half. It felt that way to him. What he felt for this girl was far more than friendship or sexual arousal. Even at their first meeting at the station, he heard his soul calling out loudly. He couldn't place it then. He was too tense before the uncertain situation he was facing.

But now, at this moment, he thought of that feeling, that call inside him, and he knew now what it meant.

Again he pressed a soft kiss to Anna's hair and nestled his cheek into her hair.

Then he closed his eyes too, his arm wrapped tightly around Anna, who was still sleeping peacefully against his chest.

Aiden startled when a hand gently stroked his upper body. He blinked a few times until he woke up properly. Anna looked at him but continued unflinchingly to explore his upper body. Again and again she lowered her head and breathed light kisses on his skin. Then she straightened up and lifted her mouth towards him, which he immediately took possession of.

And for the first time their lips opened and they played with their tongues. They probed further and further and ended in a passionate kiss that made Aiden groan.

When they looked into each other's eyes again, they spoke the same language and let them find each other again, in a stormy union of the lips.

The arousal grew and Aiden, falling more and more into excitement, searched with his hands for a patch of Anna's skin that he could feel under her blouse as he slid his hand under the fabric at her neck.

Anna sat up and slowly undid the buttons of her blouse. With flushed cheeks and a slightly embarrassed look at Aiden, she slipped off her blouse. Underneath, she wore a light vest with thin straps.

Aiden stroked the skin on her shoulders, ran his fingers tenderly over her collarbone to her neck, where the artery throbbed fiercely.

His hands moved back to her shoulders, then down to her waist and he pulled the chemise out of the waistband and immediately his hands roamed over her bare back.

Anna grabbed the bottom edge of the shirt and pulled it over her head.

Ashamed, she held the shirt in front of her bare chest.

Aiden looked at her and gently pulled the shirt out of her hand and threw it on the floor.

He stood up and pulled Anna up, took her in his arms and kissed her passionately.

His hand stroked her delicate, fine skin again, under her arms to her waist, lightly grazing the base of her breast, making her inhale audibly.

"Is that all right with you?" he whispered questioningly in her ear.

"Yes, please don't stop," she breathed in a trembling, excited voice.

Aiden lifted her in his arms and laid her on the sofa, kneeling in front of her and kissing every millimetre of her bare skin. He relied entirely on the guidance of his feelings and lust. Tenderly and without haste.

Once again he lifted his gaze to her eyes and saw the approval and excitement reflected in them, which he felt the same way.

Space and time were forgotten, there were only the two of them. Anna let him and enjoyed how much he spoiled her. Everything was so new and yet as if it had always been like this. All shyness was gone.

Everything happened so naturally and there were no more inner obstacles or barriers.

They gave themselves to each other, in perfect agreement and in shared lust that made them reach their first climax.

Some time later they were lying next to each other on the sofa, naked, exhausted and in complete contentment, holding hands. They had shared the most intimate thing two lovers can give each other. Carried by give and take. And in that moment, their love for each other ignited, knowing that they wanted to hold on to it forever, for all eternity.

When Aiden walked home late in the evening, he was filled with feelings of happiness and love, so that he hardly noticed his way, and he suddenly found himself at the front door in Agnes Street.

He looked up the wall of the house to the second floor and saw the light still burning in the living room. So Elisabeth had been waiting for him. He felt guilty that he had not told her. But he hadn't expected the day to end like this and had forgotten all about it.

*

As he entered the flat, he heard a sobbing that immediately froze him. He ran into the living room and found Elisabeth crying at the table.

"What happened, Elisabeth? I'm sorry, I couldn't let you know it was getting so late," he looked at her worriedly.

Elisabeth shook her head and wiped the tears from her cheeks.

"Greta was here earlier and made a terrible scene for me. Her boyfriend Anton was seriously injured a few days ago. She got the news today. She accused me again of not helping her, of Anton being released. It would be my fault if he possibly died."

"She's crazy, isn't she? What makes her think you would have connections to such places that could prevent someone from being released from frontline duty?"

"I think she realised that I had contact with someone who issued the new papers for you. I explained to her that this was someone from the Residents' Office and no one who had any influence on position orders or Wehrmacht justice. Of course she didn't believe me."

Elisabeth took a deep breath before continuing.

"She screamed at me that I was hiding a deserter here with me and keeping you as a young lover. I couldn't calm her down."

Aiden got wide-eyed.

"She really thinks that of you?"

"I don't know Aiden. She's gone completely mad."

"What else did she say?" he stared forebodingly at Elisabeth and dropped dejectedly into a chair.

Elisabeth burst into tears again.

"Please tell me what else Greta told you," Aiden asked her again urgently.

"That she will betray you and me if Anton should die." Her voice was only a whisper and she cupped her hands in front of her tear-soaked face.

"I didn't know what else to say. I couldn't tell her the truth, otherwise I would have only made things worse and she would certainly have sent the military justice system after us today."

Aiden's mind began to race. His pulse raced and fear crept over him.

He had to get away, as quickly as possible, was the only thought he could think at that moment.

But if he told Elisabeth this, she would not let him go, he knew that. But what should they do. They would both go to prison?

During his time at the front, he had overheard many a conversation among the other soldiers about deserters and defectors who had been caught. Up to five years in prison was written on them. And even for the people who aided and abetted these deserters, they did not get off scot-free and could get up to three years in prison.

It seemed very strange to Aiden, because he had never thought of himself as a deserter before, had never given it a thought. It was only now that he suddenly became aware of it.

He now knew he was considered nothing more than a deserter and defector who had fled to an enemy country to escape the front-line war and survive.

He saw himself simply as a man, almost a boy, who was very afraid of the cruelty he experienced there and of death. And he would probably have been dead long ago if he hadn't met Franz in that bomb hole and if he hadn't made him this proposal.

For Aiden, looking back now, it felt like everything had been controlled.

One thing led to another. It just happened, without him planning anything.

Aiden looked at Elisabeth, who was still sitting in her chair like a heap of misery and shaking her head in disbelief.

"I can't believe Greta's going so crazy," she whispered in a choked voice.

Aiden remained silent. He did not know what to say.

The thought matured in him more and more that he had to leave. He had to do it for Elisabeth. She had helped him and given him so much. He had to protect her. Too much was at stake for her.

If he disappeared and there was nothing left here to prove that she had taken in someone from the enemy camp, then at least she had a good chance of not being punished if Greta really did notify the military justice system.

He saw this as the only way to avoid disaster for Elisabeth.

"Don't worry Elisabeth, we will find a solution," he tried to reassure her, although it was anything but calm inside him.

"Yes, you're right. Now we'll go to bed and in the morning we'll talk about everything calmly. I'm sure we'll think of something.

I just don't give up hope that Greta won't go so far as to turn us in after all. Besides, she has no proof for her accusations. You have papers. even if they contain false information, they are real papers."

Elisabeth stood up and went to Aiden and took him in her arms.

"You have grown so close to my heart. You're a good boy and I want you to come back one day when the war is over. You can travel home to your family."

"Thank you Elisabeth," he returned her embrace, moved. "And I would like nothing more than for you to accompany me then, to Ireland, to my family. So that they can meet you and I can show you my beautiful country."

"Yes, we will do that, Aiden. I'm sure we will," she whispers, touched. "Good night."

"Good night, Elisabeth," he replied in a brittle voice.

He knew that there would be no reunion in the morning, for he had already made up his mind.

Elisabeth went to the door. Aiden looked sadly after her.

"Elisabeth!"

"Yes Aiden?" she replied, turning to him.

"Thank you for all you do for me."

Elisabeth looked at him with a sad but very loving smile and walked out of the room.

Aiden remained sitting in his chair. Thoughts were spinning in his head.

He had to leave. He had no choice.

Thinking of Anna, a deep pain spread through him. What should he do? Go to her and tell her everything and then say goodbye? Or tell her nothing at all and just disappear? He was lost in thought and couldn't find a solution that felt right.

Should he write her a letter and explain everything to her? However, he did not want to drag her further into this story. His arms folded on the table, he put his head in his hands and began to cry bitterly.

So he sat there for some time and let his emotions run free and finally made the decision that almost tore his heart apart. But he had no other choice if he wanted to protect the people who were so close to him. He had to disappear, immediately and silently.

*

Everything was quiet in the flat. Aiden looked out of the window. Dusk had not yet fallen. It was three o'clock in the morning. Elisabeth would not be up until six. He listened at her bedroom door. Was Anna asleep or was her preoccupation keeping her awake? But when he pressed his ear to the door, everything inside was quiet and Aiden hoped she was fast asleep.

Aiden went into his room and quickly packed up his few things and put everything into an old grey backpack.

He put on his sturdy shoes, which he had also taken from Franz's estate, and laced them up tightly and took a warm jacket from the wardrobe. He put the golden coin that he had kept safely in his bedside table into his trouser pocket. It was a little anchor for him to hold on to and he hoped he could continue to rely on it. Likewise the silver pocket watch he had received from Greta for Christmas. He could possibly sell it if he needed money.

How contradictory this was, Aiden thought.

First Greta gave him such a valuable gift and now she wanted to betray him and Elisabeth. Aiden now learned at a very young age that he had to be very careful with people and consciously watch who he could trust and who he could not. Then he went into the kitchen and made himself some sandwiches, which he wrapped in old newspaper. He took some notes from a tin box in which Elisabeth was saving some money to buy food. He hoped very much that she could forgive him for that. And then packed everything into his rucksack.

Then he looked around the living room to see if there was anything lying around that belonged to him. He took the notebooks with the German vocabulary he had studied with, the book by Oscar Wilde that Elisabeth had given him and put it all in his rucksack.

Aiden had no plan where to go or how to survive. Where he could hide? But one thing he knew for sure, he had to go.

Again and again, his thoughts revolved around Anna. His love, whom he had found here in Germany and whom he now had to leave. With a heavy heart, he had decided not to leave her a letter or an explanation. It would be better for her, he thought. His heart broke at the thought that he had to hurt her so much after she had just lost her mother. But this way, maybe she would hate him for being such a bastard and just disappearing after they had first made love. And it would be easier for her to hate him than to mourn him. That way she would be able to forget him faster. He had to deal with his own pain himself.

He was fully aware that his chances were slim of suviving to escape without being discovered.

But it was better that he be picked up somewhere alone than here with Elisabeth. He had to protect her.

However, he still hoped that Greta would calm down and leave Elisabeth in peace when he was gone. That was his one deepest wish.

With his backpack on his shoulder, he looked around once more at the flat where he had spent so much time and which had offered him security. Now he had to leave the safety and go on his way, where it would lead was written in the stars. First he had to go and then he would see.

Eyes wet with tears, he quietly closed the flat door behind him, descended the stairs and stepped out of the house onto the pavement and walked off, slowly into the dawning morning into an uncertain future.

*

Anna
Munich, November 1917

She wandered aimlessly around the English Garden. With both hands she held her much too thin coat tightly around her. She was shivering from the cold. But she hardly noticed it. She had been frozen inside for weeks and no longer felt any warmth inside her.

She could not calm down. She had just been to see Doctor Schneider, who had told her some incredible news. Still she could not believe it. She thought she felt so bad because she was in such deep grief and unspeakable sorrow that she could neither eat nor sleep. As soon as she took a few bites, she immediately threw up.

A cruel time dawned for Anna in the past weeks. Day by day she felt more miserable and exhausted and she did not know what to do next. Deep hopelessness overshadowed her soul. But the reason for her health problems was not grief and sadness alone. There was another reason, as Doctor Schneider had just told her.

She was expecting a child.

Deeply shaken, she crouched down on a park bench.

*

When Anna opened her eyes, she was lying on a park bench underneath a busy bridge, next to the Isar.

The sounds of the passing vehicles thundered in her head like hammer blows.

Where was she? How did she get here? Where was she going? Who was she anyway? What had happened? Why is she so incredibly cold?

She only came to with difficulty. She felt terribly sick. Again and again, her consciousness slipped away. But she used all the strength she could muster to stay awake. Was it only seconds that she kept drifting away, or was it minutes or even hours?

Again and again she lifted her eyelids with difficulty and saw the passing automobiles and horse-drawn carriages on the bridge in a blur, which seemed to her like flying splotches of colour, before her heavy eyelids lowered again.

Everything was going round in circles in her head. She felt like she was on a big swing, swinging back and forth and spinning in circles at the same time.

With difficulty, she made an attempt to stand up, but she did not manage it. Her legs gave way immediately and she almost fell to the ground, had it not been for an attentive pedestrian who had just passed the bench, who held her at the last moment and put her safely back on the bench.

"What's the matter with you? Are you not feeling well? Shall I call a doctor?" the somewhat older passer-by looked at her with concern.

Anna raised her head and tried to look at the old man despite the incredible dizziness, but his face blurred before her eyes. She wanted to say something, but no sound came from her lips.

Everything was paralysed, nothing worked the way she wanted it to, she felt like she was frozen. She felt trapped inside herself and could not free herself from it.

"You're frozen to the bone. Are you drunk? she heard the man's voice say, "In broad daylight, shame on you!" he exclaimed indignantly all at once and let go of her.

Before she could react in any way, the man moved on and she was alone again.

She continued to struggle with her consciousness, trying again and again to wake up from this nightmare. But again and again the dizziness hurled her like a whirlwind through different levels of consciousness.

A moment ago she was sitting on the bench, desperately holding on to it, but now she realised that she was falling, far down, until she hit her head hard on the wood of the bench. Then everything went dark around her.

"Hello, Miss....wake up. What´s you?" Again a man wrong with stood in front of the park bench and gently shook Anna's arm.

Anna opened her eyes with difficulty and was again aware of a figure leaning over her and shaking her.

She wanted to say something, but when she tried to speak, no sound came out of her mouth.

"You're half frozen," the man said. "Shall I take you home?" Anna tried again to make herself heard, but she was too weak and just wanted to sleep.

Suddenly a terrible pain shot through her lower abdomen and she writhed in pain.

Then she felt arms suddenly grab her and lift her off the bench.

Out of instinct, she wanted to fight back, but she lacked any strength to do so either and helplessly surrendered to the man's grip, sinking again into a deep swoon.

End

Where will the path lead for Aiden? Will he succeed in escaping? What choices will he make? What will become of Anna, who stays behind pregnant? And many more questions remain unanswered.

There will be a second part of the story. Be curious about what else will happen, I am too. To be honest, I don't really know the answers myself yet. They arise in me in the writing process, which makes writing as exciting for me as reading my book hopefully is for you.

I would be very happy to receive feedback on the book. Christina-maria.schweiger@t-online.de

Hint:

The story and all the characters in the story are fictional. However, the places and events in Ireland and on the Western Front in France and Belgium during the First World War did and do exist in reality. I have done my best to incorporate the facts into the story as faithfully as possible.

I went on a research trip to Belgium and drove along the front line of the time, where you can follow the history of the battles on the Western Front. Immersing yourself in this environment, marked and lined with small and large military cemeteries that tell stories, you can only imagine the war scenarios and cruelty that took place there.

In Ireland, by the sea, I often spend time and worked on my book there, but also enjoy this Irish life, as well as the people there, and will always return.

Thank you

I would like to thank my son Stefan, who helped me a lot with the correction and often assisted me with tips and valuable advice. I would also like to thank Lena O´Neill for revising the English text.

Also thanks to my test readers Gabi and Christian Markart, Claudia Hondl, Claudia Jungwirt and Stefan Schweiger for their valuable advice and motivation to continue. Many thanks to Stefan Lindner, who again so quickly and easily finished the book cover for me to print.

I would especially like to thank Michael J. Whelan, Irish author, historian and Keeper of the Irish Air Corps Military Aviation Museum & Collection, for his invaluable help in researching the Battle of the Sommé and the events of the First World War. He acted as a living encyclopaedia for me on a number of occasions with his immense knowledge. I am deeply grateful for this.

Michael J. Whelan is the author of, among other things, "The Battle of Jadotville" and his book of poetry "Peacekeeper", which led me to him.

"Let me show you the world with my eyes.", reads the introduction to his book "Peacekeeper".

For me, the eyes of a poet are the transformer of the soul.

Seeing and experiencing the war from a soldier's perspective was partly my motivation for writing the book.

It's been on my mind all my life what these men had to go through, especially in World War I, to come back broken as human beings, if they survived.